"He Can't Hurt You,
Mr. Brennan

"Not in the slightest, Miss—er—"

"Hill. It's Sidonie Hill—"

"Ah, I might have known!"

"What?"

'That you would be called Sidonie, or Prudence or Camilla, although I would have bet on Prudence," Mike Brennan responded.

"Why are you going out of your way to

LINDSAY ARMSTRONG was born in South Africa but now lives in Australia with her New Zealand-born husband and their five children. They have lived in nearly every state of Australia and tried their hand at some unusual—for them—occupations, such as farming and horse training, all grist to the mill for a writer! Lindsay started writing romances when their youngest child began school and she was left feeling at loose ends. She is still doing it and loving it.

Books by Lindsay Armstrong

HARLEQUIN PRESENTS
1593—AN UNUSUAL AFFAIR
1626—THE SEDUCTION STAKES
1656—UNWILLING MISTRESS
1693—A DIFFICULT MAN

LINDSAY ARMSTRONG

An Unsuitable Wife

Harlequin Books

TORONTO • NEW YORK • LONDON
AMSTERDAM • PARIS • SYDNEY • HAMBURG
STOCKHOLM • ATHENS • TOKYO • MILAN
MADRID • WARSAW • BUDAPEST • AUCKLAND

ISBN 0-373-11713-2

AN UNSUITABLE WIFE

Copyright © 1994 by Lindsay Armstrong.

This edition published by arrangement with Harlequin Enterprises B.V.

Printed in U.S.A.

CHAPTER ONE

SIDONIE HILL was not given to indulging in tears but that was exactly what she felt like doing as she dropped her bag to the ground and sat down wearily on a bench outside an Airlie Beach store.

Among her minor woes was the fact that she was overdressed and perspiring liberally, her major one the fact that she had just been presented with her fare home but had no home to go to, no job and no visible means of support. Not that she was entirely destitute but the *disappointment* of the whole situation was crushing as well as the fact that she couldn't afford to stay out of work for too long.

How do I get myself into these situations? she asked herself bitterly, and blinked vigorously. She was not helped in her predicament by the small inner voice that told her she was, always had been and possibly always would be, a rather impractical kind of person, nor had this been helped along by the fact that she'd been born to a brilliant but highly impractical father to whom nothing but nuclear physics had had much importance. To make matters worse, she'd lost her mother at an early age and had been reared in the rarefied atmosphere of university academic life.

And that's why, she thought gloomily, I'm *over-qualified* for this teaching job on an outback station—or was it just another way of saying they didn't like the look and the sound of me? Quite likely, she mused with a grimace, but, be that as it may, my quest for adventure has passed me by; I've burnt my boats back in Melbourne—well, to be honest I'd just hate to go back, so what do I do?

She looked around. Airlie Beach in North Queensland was possessed of that blinding kind of sunlight one associated with the tropics and thought longingly of with not the slightest understanding of how powerful and hot it was, she realised. It was also a stepping-off point from the mainland for the Whitsunday Passage and essentially a holiday town where people wore little and seemed to be a very casual, free and easy lot.

Her eyes fell on just such a group, a man and two girls standing on the pavement a few feet away. The man, who, one had to admit, was tall and beautifully proportioned, nevertheless wore ragged shorts, no shirt to obstruct one's view of his broad shoulders and sleek torso, or shoes, and his hair was longish and he had a red bandanna around it. The two girls had on bikinis beneath see-through shirts, and thongs, and were carrying small colourful holdalls; it appeared as if they were parting company, the girls from the man, because they were saying goodbye with a lot of hilarity and thanking him for a wonderful time. As a final gesture he embraced them in turn then waved them off and turned to go into the store.

It's no wonder people find the look of me strange, Sidonie reflected; I must stand out like a sore thumb. And she mused along these painful lines for a few minutes then jumped as a voice beside her said, 'Excuse me.'

It was the shirtless man who had just gone into the store and he was regarding her quizzically from a pair of very blue eyes set in a tanned, rather hawk-like face beneath his longish brown hair.

'Are you talking to me?' Sidonie enquired haughtily before she could stop herself.

'Sure am! I believe you're looking for a job?'

'I—well, yes, but what's it to you?' Sidonie gazed up at him with more than a little affront expressed in her grey eyes.

He laughed at her and his teeth were quite white and dazzling, she noted at the same time as she bristled further and stood up—causing her interrogator to frame his lips to a soundless whistle. 'Well, strike me pink,' he drawled.

'And what does that mean?' Sidonie asked through her teeth although she had to tilt her chin up because he was nearly a head taller, probably at least six feet to her five feet four, she guessed.

'I don't know,' he said pensively, those blue eyes roaming up and down her slender figure, so stiflingly dressed in a wilting heavy white cotton shirt with a tight-buttoned neckline and long sleeves, a hound's-tooth check skirt, stockings and flat black shoes. Then his eyes came back to her face, registered the total lack of make-up and he murmured, 'Just that you look hot and bothered, I guess; you have to have the palest skin in the place—which could be a problem but not insurmountable—and I don't think I've seen such lovely fair hair for a while...' He paused and grimaced. 'I haven't seen such a prim bun for years either so I think it was the combination of one up-tight, out-of-place lady that caused me to express some—amazement.'

Sidonie's very pale skin burned in a comprehensive blush and, because she was inclined to be hot-headed as well as impractical, she said tartly, 'If you think the impressions of a person such as yourself, whom one could be forgiven for confusing with a tramp——' she allowed her gaze to roam up and down him as he had done to her '—mean anything to me at all, you're much mistaken.'

'Wow!' he said softly. 'A *very* uptight lady. Is it because you're out of work?' he queried kindly.

Sidonie put her hands on her hips. 'How do *you* know I'm out of work anyway?'

He jerked his thumb over his shoulder. 'You were telling Mrs Watson in the store.'

'Oh.' It was true. She'd noticed a bulletin board in the store upon which were tacked a variety of notices such as items for sale as well as two positions vacant ones, one for a cook in a motel, one for an experienced Bobcat operator. Since she was quite sure she'd be a disaster as a cook and the wrong sex for a Bobcat operator, she'd enquired of the lady behind the counter if she knew of any other jobs available and had received the lowering information that the recession was biting so deeply that the usual flow of casual jobs such as barmaids, house maids, et cetera had quite dried up. 'Well,' she said loftily, his summing-up of her still rankling deeply, 'I have to say the mind boggles at the thought of what kind of job you might be about to offer me but I suppose I could hear you out.'

He grinned and appeared to be not one whit perturbed. 'I'm looking for crew.'

'Crew?' She frowned.

'For a boat,' he said patiently. 'A fifty-two-foot yacht I'm—breaking in for a friend. It's rather a handful on its own, you see, and my last crew have just left.'

'Those girls?'

'Uh-huh. Do you know anything about boats and sailing?'

'As a matter of fact I do,' she said slowly, then blinked confusedly and wondered if she'd gone mad. 'However, if you imagine I would even *consider* crewing for a strange man . . . I could end up heaven knows what!' she said hotly.

'Raped, murdered and your body dumped in the briny?' he said softly. 'I should tell you your kind of superior, possibly neurotic girl doesn't appeal to me in the slightest. You'd be quite safe but its entirely up to you.' He smiled at her, a singularly charming smile that reduced that hawk-like impression surprisingly, and added wryly, 'I don't know why but my good deeds have a habit of falling flat—had you noticed that about good deeds?'

'I don't know what you're talking about,' Sidonie said stiffly.

'Well, when I saw you sitting there with tears on your lashes——'

'I wasn't,' she whispered, going bright red again.

'Yes, you were. And when I found out why you were trying not to cry, I was prompted to be—philanthropic, I suppose, despite the fact that you couldn't be less my type if you tried. Oh, well,' he shrugged, 'if you change your mind, if you do have any sailing experience, Mrs Watson has all the details. But I am sailing at the crack of dawn tomorrow on the high tide. Goodbye—I hope your fortunes improve,' he said gravely, and strolled away.

* * *

Sidonie had lunch in a café in a curiously abstracted state, even for her. And at one point she thought, I can't believe I'm even thinking this! But the fact was, she couldn't seem to help it and the bevy of tanned, happy, skimpily clad people about her were, in a curious way, urging her on.

And when she'd spun out her lunch as long as she could, she found herself turning in the direction of Mrs Watson's general store...

'Mike Brennan, you mean?' Mrs Watson said and sighed with pleasure. 'Oh, he's a lovely man!'

'Well, I didn't quite mean in that respect—is he reliable, respectable—that kind of thing?'

'So far as I know.' Mrs Watson opened her eyes wide. 'He's been coming up here for a few years now and I don't know of any complaints. The opposite if anything; everyone seems to like him. And he's a really good customer and he often brings me back some fish. Oh, no, he's nice all right!'

'Where does he come from?'

'Somewhere down south,' Mrs Watson said vaguely.

'Well...' Sidonie hesitated '...what does he do?'

'Something to do with boats, I believe—oh, Jim——' she looked past Sidonie to the policeman who had just come in '—this young lady is making enquiries about Mike Brennan, how respectable he is and so on.'

'Mike Brennan?' Jim said with a lift of his eyebrow. 'One of the best if you ask me. Why?'

'I think he's asked her to crew on his boat,' Mrs Watson murmured.

If she'd said Mike Brennan had asked a baby elephant to crew on his boat, Jim the policeman could not have expressed more surprise in a mostly silent way. His wide-eyed gaze roamed up and down Sidonie, his mouth opened to make some startled exclamation but he shut it sharply then coughed.

Sidonie closed her own eyes and counted to ten beneath her breath. Then she said tautly, 'I should have thought it was only prudent to make some enquiries before one sailed off with a man one had never met before, however——'

'Oh, it is,' Jim said hastily. 'Very wise indeed. So what can I tell you? Mike is an expert sailor and I've never had one word of complaint from anyone who's crewed for him over the years, nor from anyone he deals with here, chandlers et cetera. Uh—naturally——' He paused and looked at her probingly.

'You can't absolutely guarantee he won't be tempted to take advantage of me?' Sidonie queried with asperity.

'Well, no,' Jim said seriously. 'But I have my doubts it would be a problem. I mean to say...' he paused again '...he——'

'I know what you're trying to say,' Sidonie interrupted. 'He himself told me I couldn't be less his type if I tried.'

'I was actually going to say I don't *think* he's the kind of bloke who presses his attentions where they're not wanted. There are also plenty of girls who—uh——' Jim grimaced and Mrs Watson tried to look serious but failed.

'Who would queue up for his attentions?' Sidonie supplied sardonically. 'I can't imagine why he doesn't get one of them, then, or two or three.'

'He could be wanting a break from that kind of thing, love,' Mrs Watson said brightly.

Sidonie regarded them both somewhat balefully and then did the silliest thing. 'All *right*. I can't think what else to do at the moment but if any harm comes to me be it on your heads!' And she carted herself and her bag, which was beginning to feel as heavy as lead, out of the store with this parting shot.

She stopped on her way down to the marina at another general store, a very general store, where she made several purchases. A shady white linen hat, a powerful sunscreen and a couple of colourful T-shirts. She paused at a rack of bikinis but reminded herself she did have a swimsuit in her bag, a rather aged, very plain navy blue garment, and told herself it would have to do. But, out on the pavement again, she suddenly changed her mind and went back in and bought not one but two bikinis, a bright red one and a hyacinth-blue one with white flowers on it. She then took herself to the park bordering the beach and sat down on a bench because her heart was beating uncomfortably and she was very much afraid she'd been extremely rash.

As she pondered this, she made the startling discovery that she'd been goaded into splurging her slender resources on bikinis of all things out of sheer pique. As a shot in the eye for all those who had made her feel entirely unattractive, and there'd been three of them, she mused ruefully, in the space of one day. But of course the larger issue, she reminded herself, was, was she going to go through with this?

She stared unseeingly at the vista before her then her eyes focused on the boats anchored off the shore; she drank in the wonderful view of the waters of the Whitsunday Passage—and before she could take issue with herself further she jumped up and began the half-hour hike to the Abel Point Marina.

'Mike Brennan? Yes, that's his boat, *Morning Mist*, over there. He—uh—expecting you?'

Sidonie looked sternly at the marina manager. 'I'm crewing for him,' she said equally sternly and was moved to add, 'Now I'm sure that might cause you some mirth but I'm in fact very good at it. Would *you* be so good as to as to stop staring at me with your mouth open and let me on to his jetty?'

Morning Mist was a sleek, beautiful ketch painted the palest grey with navy trim and her skipper was lounging in the cockpit drinking beer from a bottle.

'Good lord,' he said as she dumped her bag on the jetty, 'so it is true!'

'What is true?' Sidonie queried stiffly.

'That you're going to do it.' Mike Brennan put his bottle down and studied her quizzically. He had donned a faded blue T-shirt but otherwise looked exactly the same.

'I don't know what you mean—how did you know anyway?' She stared at him nonplussed.

'I received a visit from the local constabulary a short while ago,' he said gravely. 'Who informed me that I'd better take the greatest care of you or else!'

Sidonie blinked. 'Jim?'

'Jim,' he agreed with some irony.

She tried to shrug offhandedly. 'It's only what a sensible person would do, I should imagine.'

'Oh, of course.'

'Have I offended you, Mr Brennan?' Sidonie then said tartly.

'Not in the slightest, Miss—er——'

'Hill. It's Sidonie Hill——'

'Ah, I might have known.'

'What?'

'That you would be called Sidonie or Prudence or Camilla, although I would have bet on Prudence.'

'I have offended you,' Sidonie said flatly.

'Why should I be offended? As a matter of fact Jim often stops by for beer.'

'Then why are you going out of your way to insult me?'

'I don't think,' he said musingly, 'it's an insult to be called prudent by name or nature.'

'It most certainly is,' she replied vigorously, 'the way you do it! Look,' she added, 'I'm very hot, I'm tired, I've been carting my bag around for hours and it wouldn't be far from the truth to say that I'm nearly at the end of my tether one way or another, so do you want me to crew on your wretched boat or do you not?'

He regarded her entirely enigmatically for a long moment—her heated face, the damp curly wisps of hair coming adrift from her bun, the quite inappropriate clothes she was wearing. Then he surprised the life out of her by saying, 'It would be an honour to have you crew on my boat, Sidonie Hill.' And he vaulted over the handrail lightly and landed beside her on the jetty. 'Welcome aboard. I'll bring your bag up.'

'Well?'

Sidonie looked around again. The interior of *Morning Mist* was deeply comfortable and wood-panelled with a jade-green carpet and padded velour seats in a matching jade with a tiny black dot. One such seat curved around a dining table and opposite was another, sofa-length and strategically placed for viewing television. The galley was probably a cook's dream with a long island bench separating it from the main living area. There were two sleeping cabins, one fore, one aft, and they both had showers and toilets. But, apart from all the dark-panelled and jade splendour, it looked lived-in. There were polished brass lamps and full bookshelves, there was a bowl of fruit on the island bench, a compact disc player beside the television, and several maps and familiar instruments strewn over the chart table.

Her eyes came back to rest on Mike Brennan's face. 'It's very nice,' she said briskly. 'What instruments do you carry, Mr Brennan?'

He lifted an eyebrow. 'I think you'd better call me Mike—uh—radar, GPS, auto-pilot; twenty-seven meg, VHF as well as Single Side Band for radios, Auto-Seaphone and the motor is a Gardiner.'

Sidonie's grey eyes suddenly shone with enthusiasm. 'Lovely,' she said with a sigh. 'I had something to do with a very old Gardiner once but it was a gem. GPS? Do you know I've always been fascinated by satellite navigation—I know the old salts think they're expensive toys but I think it's thrilling!'

He said nothing for a moment but there was no disguising the surprise in his eyes. 'So you do know something about it?'

'Quite a bit,' she confided. 'My boyfriend and I used to do a lot of sailing on Port Phillip Bay—that's off Melbourne——'

'I have had some experience of Port Phillip Bay,' he murmured.

'Then you'll know it's no kindergarten!'

'Definitely not,' he agreed and narrowed his eyes. 'What does your boyfriend have to say about you doing this?'

Sidonie sobered. 'He's no longer my—that.'

'Why?'

Sidonie stared at him haughtily. He shrugged and a wry smile twisted his lips. 'You might as well tell me. What possible harm could it do?'

She frowned then said reluctantly, 'I suppose you're right—although I don't think crewing means I should have to bare my heart to you or that kind of thing. I——'

'By no means. OK, it's up to you.'

Sidonie thought for a bit then she said matter-of-factly, 'He fell in love with someone else, someone who was all the things I'm not, I guess, although she's hopeless on boats, but then again...I don't know why I'm telling you all this.' She shrugged ruefully. 'It must be to do with having had an extremely trying day!'

Mike Brennan tried not to smile. 'Do you drink?' he queried.

'Very rarely—what's that got to do with it?'

'Sometimes it helps. Why don't you also take the weight off your feet?' He pointed to a bar stool and went behind the island bench.

Which was how, several minutes later, Sidonie came to have in her hand a glass full of a lovely chilled white wine and before her on the bench a bowl of walnuts and olives.

Mike Brennan waited until she'd sipped some wine before he said, 'How come it's been such an unusually trying day?'

Sidonie put her glass down regretfully. 'Well, I applied for a job up here—not precisely here but at a small outback school on a large cattle property. They seemed very impressed with my credentials and they paid for me to fly up for an interview so I——' she paused and grimaced '—I rather assumed the job was in the bag so to speak.'

'It wasn't?'

She sighed. 'They took one look at me and...came to the conclusion I wouldn't suit although what they told me was I was over-qualified for it.'

'Over-qualified to be a teacher?'

'Yes. Well, I must admit I haven't had a lot of *experience* at it,' she said ruefully. 'The one job I did have in that line—er—wasn't entirely successful but I'm quite convinced the school was more to blame than I was.'

Several expressions chased through Mike Brennan's blue eyes but he said soberly enough, 'What did you do?'

'I——' Sidonie glanced at him cautiously '—I taught them to play poker. At the same time I was teaching them English,' she hastened to add.

'How old were they?' he said in the same sober way.

'Seven and eight.'

He burst out laughing.

'It's not really funny,' Sidonie remarked reproachfully. 'Their English improved dramatically as it happened.'

'I don't quite see the connection,' he said, still grinning.

'It's simple.' She looked surprised. 'We would only have a game if *everyone* had done their homework and concentrated properly in the lesson.'

'Quite simple,' he marvelled. 'But the school didn't approve?'

Sidonie sighed again. 'They said I could be turning them into compulsive gamblers.'

'What a prospect—you might have been better with Snap and Happy Families.'

Sidonie shrugged. 'That's another of my contentions that they didn't agree with—I think children are often a lot brighter than they're given credit for.'

'Well, I agree with you there, but you didn't actually use money—or did you?'

'Oh, no, we used broad beans.'

He grinned and offered her an olive.

'Thanks.' She bit into it reflectively. 'So.'

He raised an eyebrow. 'So? Your teaching experience sounds not only limited but disastrous yet you were quite sure you would get this job—forgive me but that sounds a bit rash.'

'It was,' Sidonie agreed gloomily. 'But I really wanted to get out of Melbourne and...' She trailed off and sipped some more wine.

'What are these over-qualifications you have?'

She brightened. 'A BA—I actually majored in English Literature—and a Bachelor of Science.'

'I'm impressed,' Mike Brennan murmured. 'But it seems a rather unusual combination.'

'Unfortunately——' Sidonie looked wry '—I'm rather unusual. If you must know I quite often feel a bit of a freak and never more so than today,' she added with a grimace. 'But I can assure you it's possible to be interested in science *and* arts.'

'I do apologise, I didn't mean to sound patronising,' he said gravely. 'Perhaps you should pursue the scientific side—career-wise, that is—rather than the educational side.'

'I was,' she said briefly.

'So?'

'I was bored to tears,' she said solemnly.

'That doesn't—does that make sense in light of what you've just told me?' he queried wryly.

'Probably not.' She drained her glass. 'It all rather goes back to my father, who died fairly recently. He was a nuclear physicist, you see, and he could never understand why mechanics was my forte. And when I wanted to get out of the laboratory and actually work among motorbikes and so on—they really fascinate me mechanically—he got very upset. He said it was no job for a girl, which was really strange because he'd always treated me as a son until then.' She blinked away a tear. 'So I stayed on, well, with just that one stint teaching—he didn't mind that—until he died. I do beg your pardon.' She drew a hanky from her pocket and blew her nose. 'I'm normally not in the least emotional.'

Mike Brennan said thoughtfully, 'Losing your father and your boyfriend can be emotional experiences, I should imagine. But what's stopping you working with motorbikes now?'

Sidonie twisted her hanky. 'Everyone I approached laughed at me.'

Mike Brennan laughed himself. 'I wonder why?' he murmured and poured her another glass of wine.

Sidonie looked down at herself. 'I know why,' she said with gentle melancholy and reflected that if one glass of wine made her feel this sorry for herself she ought not to have any more, but it was oddly comforting to be able to be so honest. 'There just doesn't seem to be a role in life for me.'

'At—twenty or so...' he hazarded, 'I wouldn't regard it as a blight on your life yet.'

'Twenty-three,' Sidonie said drily, 'and that's the kind of facile thing people say but I do assure you it's no help at all.'

He looked at her thoughtfully, not in least perturbed by her intended slight, apparently, then he said idly, 'Could I make a less facile suggestion? Don't wear your hair like that, throw away those clothes—and life might just surprise you, Sidonie Hill.'

'Ah,' Sidonie responded. 'No, it wouldn't. It's still the same me, you see. Just as you would probably be highly uncomfortable in anything other than shorts and a T-shirt, and with a decent haircut, I wouldn't be any less *me*. And if you were implying that men might be tempted to take more of an interest in me were I to do those things you suggested—two points.' She gestured and reached for her glass. 'Life might certainly surprise me but would it actually improve? I wonder——'

He broke in with a half-smile, 'Why shouldn't it? Or do you have something against men finding you attractive?'

'Not the *right* man, no.' It was her turn to look faintly quizzical. 'They don't seem to be too thick on the ground, however. But you know, it's not so much *men*—or the lack of them—that bothers me. It's—this lack of purpose, not being able to find the right job, the right niche. That's what really bothers me.'

'On the other hand, is that not why you left Melbourne? Because of your failed—relationship?'

Sidonie frowned. 'Well, obviously it was one reason. It's not very pleasant to be thrown over for another woman; I can't deny that it made a bit of a dent in my self-esteem but I've got the feeling it might not have worked anyway.'

'And why is that?' Mike Brennan queried with a straight face.

Sidonie chewed her lip. 'I know it sounds odd and what I really mean is this, I think...' She paused. 'We were good friends and perhaps we confused that with being in love. It was certainly all very nice and comfortable but when he fell in love with this other girl it sort of dawned on me that there'd been no real *passion* in our relationship. No heart-stirring stuff, no feeling breathlessly happy and not wanting to be away from each other for a moment. Which is how he felt about her,' she said ruefully. 'And of course I was then led to wonder whether I was capable of inducing that kind of thing in a man. It's not always a help to be interested in the kind of things I am, from a man's point of view, I'm beginning to perceive. I think, speaking very generally, of course, men still prefer women to be very feminine.'

'And you don't think you are?' Mike Brennan said in a totally deadpan way.

'Not *outwardly*,' Sidonie replied, her brow furrowed as she concentrated. 'Take my choice in clothes for one thing—I'm really happiest in a pair of overalls so I never bother much about them and when I do I never get it right. I have a lot of trouble with my hair, I——' But she hesitated and stopped, thinking that her other major shortcoming might be better kept a secret until there was no turning back. So she said instead, 'Do you know what I mean at all?' and winced when she thought she saw a glint of compassion in his eyes and said hastily, 'It doesn't really matter. As I said earlier, it's not my *main* cause of concern.'

He looked at her thoughtfully for a long moment. 'As a matter of fact I agree with you,' he said finally. 'To the extent that the outward manifestations of one's femininity, or masculinity for that matter, may not always be a true guide.'

'Oh, I'm so relieved to hear you say so!' Sidonie smiled at him widely and then was struck by an awful thought which caused her to start to colour and add disjointedly, 'Not...I mean...not in any personal sense, of course! Just that it reflects that you could be a thinking, fairly intelligent sort of person... Oh, dear,' she wound down unhappily, 'perhaps I should say no more.'

'Perhaps,' he agreed but with a wicked little glint of amusement dancing in his eyes. 'But until you make up your mind on my intelligence or otherwise, may I make a *practical* suggestion this time? Why don't you unpack, have a shower and change? You don't need to be careful of water while we're in the marina; I'll fill up again before we go—and I'll start dinner. The sun has slipped past the yard arm, in case you hadn't noticed.'

Half an hour later Sidonie emerged from the forward cabin a bit hesitantly. The shower had been wonderful, the cabin, although small, had ample space for her possessions and she'd changed into a pair of white shorts and one of the T-shirts she'd bought. She'd also washed her hair and plaited it. The aromas coming from the galley were delicious, but despite all this she couldn't help but be struck by the thought that she'd committed herself to sharing a very confined space with a total stranger and she didn't even know for how long.

So she was quiet as they ate grilled lamb chops, a potato casserole topped with cheese and tomato, and fresh green beans, followed by a fresh fruit salad and cream. She also declined any more wine and was just gearing herself up to ask some pertinent questions when Mike Brennan pushed away his dessert plate and said idly, 'I'd guess you'd like to know my plans.'

'Oh. Yes,' she replied gratefully.

'Know anything about the Whitsunday area?'

'No,' she confessed. 'Not a lot. I boned up on cattle and cattle stations et cetera—I'm actually a walking mine of information on different breeds...Simmental, Poll Herefords, Charolais as well as artificial insemination and the like, which was a bit of a waste of time as it's turned out although they say knowledge can never be useless—but I wasn't expecting to be out on the water.'

'Well, come and have a look at the map,' he said, again looking wickedly amused, and a moment later was showing her the main islands in the area. 'Hayman, Hook, Whitsunday, Haslewood, Hamilton all have protected anchorages, so what I plan is a leisurely cruise around them for a couple of weeks and then I'll be taking her down to Tin Can Bay, which is to be her home base.' His finger moved a long way down the map and Sidonie's eyes widened.

His own eyes narrowed faintly as he watched her and he said after a moment, 'That will be something for us to make a mutual decision about—whether you come that far or I drop you back here.'

'I see.' She thought for a bit and looked around. 'It looks brand-new, this boat.'

'It is. There are only about twenty hours on the log, which is why I decided to take on crew. There are inevitably teething problems on new boats and it's handy to have someone else on board.'

'I would have thought you needed a man.'

'As a matter of fact I've had some excellent crew, sailing-wise, who were girls, although none with your mechanical experience. And even if they can't sail it's a great help to have someone to cook when things are going wrong.'

'I see,' Sidonie said again, mentally digesting this and wondering what else those girls had been good at.

'What you're wondering now, my friend Sidonie,' he said with a tinge of irony, 'doesn't sit that well with the sentiments you expressed earlier.'

Sidonie raised her expressive grey eyes to his and there was a certain cool hauteur in them. 'No? Which sentiments were those?'

'That women can be good at all sorts of things, as you yourself are, and men should be able to accept that and see beyond the frills and furbelows. At least I think that's what you were trying to say.'

'Ah,' she murmured, not lowering her gaze by a fraction, 'I was. I was not, however, to be seen kissing you in public this morning or, more to the point, being kissed *by* you after crewing on your boat.'

A look of exasperation tempered by some devilish humour came to his expression. 'All the same I didn't sleep with them; they were only on board for the trip down from Townsville where I ... where the boat was bought, and because they were sweet, nice kids who'd enjoyed every minute of their adventure, and because I know one of their brothers rather well, I kissed them goodbye. Furthermore, in case you weren't aware of it, it was not the kind of kissing lovers indulge in;

people are very informal in this part of the world and among the boating fraternity, Miss Hill; and if those kind of quite innocent things are going to shock you all the time, we may have to rethink our...association.'

'It's up to you,' Sidonie said levelly. 'I just like to get things quite clear in my mind,' she added.

He stared at her then shook his head wryly. 'I've got the feeling whatever I say will be taken down and used in evidence against me but for what it's worth here goes—I did have a friend, the brother I mentioned a moment ago, lined up for these sea trials but he broke a leg a couple of days ago. That's how I came to be reduced to seeking strange crew, little to know how strange they were going to be,' he said with a lethal kind of gentleness. 'However, I have, over the years of cruising in yachts, used women crew—even strange women crew at times, which I would have thought merely demonstrated that I'm not a male chauvinist. Only to discover——' his lips twisted '—that it has caused you to feel sure it's a deep, devious ploy to lure them into my bed.'

Sidonie raised an eyebrow. 'Can you tell me it's never happened?'

'Yes, I can,' he replied equably but with less latent humour. 'In fact I can go further and say quite catagorically that I have never asked any woman to step on board any boat with an ulterior motive in mind. You're quite safe, Sidonie, but of course I can only say it; whether you believe me or not is up to you.'

Sidonie pursed her lips then said at length, 'All right, I'll accept that with the proviso that you also promise no ulterior motives develop later on——' He swore beneath his breath, but she continued doggedly,

'And I refuse to be embarrassed about any of this despite your efforts to make me feel so.'

Mike Brennan stared at her for a full minute, looking every bit as hawkish as he was capable of, but Sidonie's gaze didn't falter. Finally a reluctant and dry little smile twisted his lips as he said, 'Why do I have the impression that if anyone's biting off more than they can chew it's *me*?'

For the first time a spark of humour lit Sidonie's eyes although she replied gravely, 'I have no idea.'

'I wonder.' He paused, seemed about to say more then changed the subject. 'I'll give you a guided tour of the galley, the freezers, fridges, et cetera, and how they operate. I think that might be enough for tonight. Would one day on, one day off suit you?'

'What——? I don't——'

'I mean that we split galley duties between us day by day.'

'Oh! Uh—yes, that would be fine,' she said and hoped it didn't sound as lame to him as it did to her. But he merely gave her a guided tour of all the facilities—the gas stove and conventional oven, the microwave oven, the ice-making machine and so on. There was no doubt that *Morning Mist* had virtually everything that opened and shut, not that those facilities were generally of much help to Sidonie—But I'll think about that tomorrow, she told herself as she unsuccessfully tried to stop yawning and battled the onset of extreme weariness.

Eventually he said, 'Mmm ... I think you'd better go to bed, Sidonie, before you fall asleep standing up. And I'll cook tomorrow—you can get acquainted with the motor and the sails if you like.'

'Thanks,' she said really gratefully. 'I do seem to be very tired although don't think I tire *easily*. I'm as strong as a horse normally; it's just that——' She stopped and coloured.

'You've had a tough day,' he supplied with a suppressed smile.

'Yes ... Goodnight,' she said uncertainly.

He studied her for a moment and she couldn't read his expression at all. Then he said quietly, 'Goodnight, Sid. Sleep well; you really don't have a thing to worry about.'

Which was how she came to fall asleep with some confusion among her thoughts—such as the rough diamond she'd assumed was Mike Brennan might not be so rough after all, and wondering how old he was and deciding he must be in his middle thirties but being unable to decide why this should concern her at all. Such as wondering how she was going to tell him that in one respect, at least, she was an utter fraud ...

CHAPTER TWO

'How's that?'

'It's really excellent. She sails like a dream!' Sidonie said enthusiastically. 'Wouldn't you just love to *own* a boat like this?'

Mike Brennan shrugged non-committally. They'd cleared the Abel Point Marina and Pioneer Rocks very early and were sailing down the Whitsunday Passage in light conditions, and added to the magic of *Morning Mist* there was a slight haze in the air so that the passage looked ethereally lovely in the morning light, a serenade of pale blues, sky and water with the islands appearing insubstantial and as if they were floating themselves. Two dolphins had accompanied them for a time, rubbing their backs under the bow of the boat then curving out of the water joyfully.

Sidonie had been aware as they'd hoisted sail and cut the motor that she'd been under Mike Brennan's hawk-like scrutiny, and aware that she'd passed his unspoken test, which had given her a curiously joyful little lift herself. Not that she'd ever handled a boat this size before, with its impressive spread of sail, but the rudiments were always the same, and she thought her father, who had taught her to sail, would have been proud of her. Then she thought of Peter Matthews, who had also been impressed by her sailing abilities, and the many happy days they'd spent together on Port Phillip Bay, and blinked a couple of times. Why didn't I realise until it was too late? she asked herself. I mean realise that what we shared wasn't the stuff dreams are made of? If only I had I could have spared myself the indignity if nothing else of having to be *told* he'd fallen in love with someone else. Perhaps even spared him the embarrassment of it all...

'Penny for them?' the tall man beside her said quietly.

'Er——' She jumped and looked at him ruefully. 'Oh, nothing really.'

'It's a shame to be sad on a morning like this.'

'You're right, it is. I'll stop!'

He smiled briefly. 'Would some breakfast help?'

'It certainly would.'

'Well, if you keep her on this course, I'll do the necessary. Are you a big breakfast eater?'

'Oh, no. What do you usually have?'

'Muesli and fruit, toast and coffee.'

'So do I!'

'Well, I'm glad we've found a couple of things in common,' he said, but nicely, and disappeared down the ladder.

I think he *is* nice, Sidonie found herself reflecting as she held *Morning Mist* on course with her sails nicely filled. She was not to know that while Mike Brennan could undoubtedly be nice he could also get extremely angry in a very cold and cutting manner...

That discovery came to her the next evening after another lovely day's sailing, when they were anchored in Stonehaven Bay off Hook Island. Not only had they had a great sail but after they'd anchored he'd lowered the dinghy and taken her coral viewing per medium of a coral viewer held into the water over the side of the dinghy, and she'd been amazed and thrilled at the colourful sight. She'd even said it reminded her of buried treasure and he'd raised an eyebrow and agreed that it was a good description.

Unfortunately, after that, she'd been unable to put off the evil moment any longer—her turn to cook dinner. Breakfast had been a breeze, lunch fairly simple—even she couldn't do much wrong with cold meat and salad—but there was plump fresh chicken reposing in the fridge awaiting her attentions, and she got a sinking feeling every time she thought about it.

Fortunately, or so she thought at the time, one of the other boats anchored in Stonehaven was known to Mike and when he was invited aboard for a drink and asked her if she'd like to go as well she'd declined and said she would rather start dinner, thinking that she'd be much better off without him breathing down her neck.

She wasn't. Despite a cook book she found—or, as she later heard herself say, actually *because* of it. She certainly wouldn't have been as adventurous without it but when there was cauliflower crying out for a white sauce and the instructions for it, a recipe for honeyed carrots... The list went on.

None of this altered the fact that, an hour and a half later when Mike Brennan returned to the boat, she'd got herself into an unbelievable, not to mention dangerous mess and had just managed to tilt the roasting tray, complete with burnt chicken, pumpkin and potatoes, so that all its contents had slid to the galley floor.

The first words he spoke she heard quite clearly although she couldn't quite see him through the smoky black haze that filled the boat.

He said, 'My God...!' Then, 'Just what the bloody hell do you think you're doing, Sidonie? Trying to burn the boat to the waterline?'

'No, no!' She gasped and coughed then yelped as she burnt herself on the roasting tray.

The next few minutes were confused and not helped by the white sauce, which quadrupled its volume into a billowing, bubbly head and cascaded all over the top of the stove, thereby adding another smell of burning of a slightly different but equally unpleasant nature.

It was only after Mike Brennan had managed to reduce the haze by opening every porthole and hatch that he stopped swearing. Then he surveyed her with blazing blue eyes but said in a voice like ice, 'How did this *happen*?'

Sidonie wiped her watering eyes and thought briefly. 'Food and I don't get along too well. I mean, I enjoy eating it well enough, there are some things I *love*, but I'm just not very good at... cooking it. Although I followed the instructions to a T, I do assure you!'

'You thoughtless, stupid, pedantic, tiresome little girl—why didn't you just *tell* me you couldn't cook?' he ground out through his teeth. 'Not only could you have burnt the boat but it will take a week to clean up the mess.'

Sidonie thought again although she felt a bit fearful and looked it. 'I don't understand *why* I can't cook, you see. And I really thought that without you around to give me an inferiority complex, plus the help of this recipe book, I might just get it right this time.'

He said something extremely uncomplimentary towards her thought processes and added that he hoped she was as good at cleaning up messes as she was at creating them, but when she assured him eagerly that she was he glared at her in a way that made her quake inside, and turned away in disgust.

They worked together for over an hour in a cold, absolutely demoralising silence. Then he said curtly, 'Leave it now, Sidonie. For one thing I'm tired of tripping over you—go and have a shower or something. I'll make us something to eat.'

She opened her mouth but received such a devastating blue glance that she closed it and turned away defeatedly.

He'd made them scrambled eggs with smoked salmon, she discovered when she nerved herself to leave her cabin, washed and cleaned up but feeling like an incredible fool.

She also discovered she was still in Coventry as they ate, and for once she could think of not a thing to say or do to ease the situation.

Then he broke the silence to say with considerable irony, 'Would I be wrong in surmising your ex boyfriend's *new* girlfriend possesses some culinary skills?'

Sidonie winced and looked away. Don't cry, she warned herself. However hurtful, it was still a horrible thing to say.

'Sidonie?'

'I don't really know. Probably,' she said gruffly and concentrated on the last little bit of smoked salmon.

'Probably,' he marvelled. 'Even if it were a bare modicum it would have to be an improvement on you.'

She didn't answer but put her knife and fork together and went to get up but flinched as the inside of her forearm came into contact with the edge of the table. She didn't see him frown and looked up in surprise when he took her wrist and turned her arm to the light, exposing the nasty little burn she'd received from the roasting dish.

Their gazes caught and held and he said in a different voice, 'Why didn't you tell me?'

'About this?'

'Yes, about this burn,' he said deliberately, still holding her wrist.

'I...I don't really know,' she murmured. 'I suppose because I'd created enough havoc without adding to it. But it's nothing,' she assured him. 'I——'

'Stop right there, Sidonie,' he warned. 'I know damn well it must have been hurting like hell and still is, and if there's one thing I don't appreciate it's false bravery——'

'It's not *false*——'

'It's not hurting?' he shot at her.

'Well . . .' she bit her lip '. . . only a little. And if you must know,' she continued, 'if you hadn't made me feel entirely as if I'd crawled out from under a stone, I would have asked you for something to put on it. I don't believe in false bravery either.'

He moved his fingers on her wrist so that she flinched again, then he raised his eyes heavenwards in total exasperation. 'Just promise me one thing, Sidonie.'

She looked at him wide-eyed. He surveyed her upturned face and wide eyes for a moment then shook his head and said merely, 'Don't talk the hind leg off a donkey until my mood improves.' And he gave her back her wrist and motioned her to sit down, whereupon he brought out a first-aid kit and dealt with her burn competently and clinically. Then he made them some coffee but declined her offer to do the dishes. 'Although,' he said meditatively, 'I think that will have to be the division of labour from hereon in. I'll be chief cook and you can be chief bottle washer.'

'Thank you very much,' she said with a rush of gratitude. 'I can't tell you how sorry I am. And tomorrow I'll clean every crevice so that it will all look like new again. Unless . . .' She paused and eyed him warily.

He narrowed his eyes. 'What?'

'I just wondered if it would be possible to teach me a bit of cookery, seeing as you seem to be so very good at it.'

He eyed her over the rim of his cup. 'How come no one else has been able to teach you?'

'No one's ever tried. Dad and I always lived on campus, you see. Oh, we had a self-contained flatlet but it was much easier to eat in the canteen.'

Mike Brennan put down his cup and stared into it silently but when she thought he wasn't going to say anything and had begun to wish she'd never mentioned the subject he looked up at last with something wry and quizzical in his eyes. 'I suppose one could only try,' he said gravely. 'If nothing else it might render you more marriageable.'

The glow that had started to light Sidonie's face up faltered and he grimaced, stood up and patted her on the head. 'Don't look like that, kid. I'm still recovering from the shock of your little débâcle—yes, I'll teach you how to cook, if it's possible.'

With that she had to be content, and discovered, curiously, that she was. And even more so when, after he'd dealt with the dishes, he put some music on the

CD, a lovely Enya album, and brought out the manual for the instrument known colloquially as a GPS, short for Global Positioning System. In fact it would have been true to say she was entranced as he explained the finer points of satellite navigation and how the instrument locked into several satellites and was thereby able to record the boat's position so that they could plot it on a chart and know exactly where they were as well as being able to put in a destination point and have it tell them the course to steer to get to it, the range in nautical miles and the time it would take to get there.

And within a very short time she had a complete grasp of the instrument, causing him to say with a lifted eyebrow, 'You may not be able to cook, friend Sid, but you've picked all this up in record time.'

Nothing diminished her glow of pleasure this time and she went to bed not long afterwards in a more contented frame of mind than one would have thought possible considering she'd nearly burnt the boat down. And as she listened to the gentle slap of the bow wave against the hull and snuggled beneath the covers her thoughts once again turned to Mike Brennan, a man she knew so little about yet was coming to like a lot.

It was at this point that it occurred to her again that while he might look like a rough diamond he didn't sound like one nor behave like one and was even looking less and less like one on closer inspection. In fact, although she wouldn't call him handsome, she decided, those aquiline features appealed to her, at least his brown hair was shiny and clean, and he did things on the boat with an economy and precision of movement, a fine-tuning of his superb physique, those broad shoulders, lean torso and long legs that was a pleasure to watch and even made her heart beat a little oddly sometimes. Then there was the way he cooked and the things he cooked and the music he liked and the books he read—you could almost be forgiven for thinking he was educated and cultured, she mused. And there was now the conundrum to add to all this that, despite her early doubts and despite incurring his dire wrath, she felt strangely safe with Mike Brennan...

The weather turned against them over the next few days. It was windy and wet, and they had a few exhilarating sails both clad in yellow rain-jackets, but when the wind rose to above twenty-five knots they sought protection in a secluded anchorage and spent two nights there until the weather eased. They were to turn into two of the happiest days Sidonie had known for a while, for several reasons. For one thing he cut down an ancient set of overalls for her and together they clambered down beneath the floorboards and inspected every part of the boat's machinery minutely and she was able to exhibit her knowledge of diesel engines and run her hands lovingly over the Gardiner as well as attend to it where required. She was also able to squeeze into impossibly small spaces, spaces he couldn't get into, and it was she who discovered the bilge pump that was not operating properly and was able to take it apart and fix it.

And although he didn't say a lot she could see from the wry look he occasionally directed her way that she sometimes amazed him, sometimes amused him.

Then there were the evenings when the wind was howling through the halyards but they were snuggly battened down and he commenced his cooking lessons. They seemed to get into a routine. They showered and changed then she perched on a stool on the other side of the island bench from him and under his direction chopped, peeled and prepared. That was all she did the first night but she listened minutely as he explained what he was doing—pot roasting a piece of blade beef, sealing in the juices by searing it first then laying it on a bed of the vegetables she'd done with a little bit of liquid, seasoning and some red wine and setting it to simmer covered until done.

'Very healthy and economical,' he commented, pouring her a glass of wine.

'Why?'

'Well, you're cooking everything in one pot on one burner and none of the goodness of the vegetables is lost because you use the liquid it's cooking in as a thin gravy.'

'I would never have thought of that. How do you know so much about it? Are you self-taught?'

'More or less.'

'That's what I thought I could be,' she said with a grimace. 'It obviously didn't work in my case.'

He smiled faintly. 'Once some of the basics become clear to you, you could surprise yourself.'

But it was the next night that he surprised her. This time they were cooking the sweetlip he'd caught earlier; he'd shown her how to fillet it, how to make a light batter and they were intending to pan fry the fillets in olive oil. The wind had dropped but it was raining heavily, the lamps were on, and for the first time she'd left her hair loose to dry after getting caught in a shower while she'd checked that the anchor was holding; it was simply parted on the side and hanging to her shoulders. It was almost dry as she concentrated carefully on the potatoes she was slicing for chips. And when she looked up once it was to find him staring at her with a faint frown.

Her eyes widened. 'Something wrong?'

'No. Why on earth do you always scrape your hair back in a pigtail or a bun?'

She put a hand to her hair self-consciously. Its colour was fine, the palest gold in fact, its texture strong and vibrant, but left to itself the ends curled riotously. 'Isn't it a terrible mess?'

'The kind of mess women pay fortunes to induce in their hair,' he said ironically.

Sidonie stared at him, her lips parted. 'Are you *sure*?' she said after a moment.

His blue eyes roamed her face and she could see a kind of wry exasperation in them as he said, 'Don't you ever look at other women?'

'Of course. Well, I must, mustn't I?'

'Then how come you've failed to realise that you have an almost perfectly oval face, beautiful eyes, skin like pale velvet, an amazingly stern little mouth when you want it to be but pink and inviting at other times— and that heavy mass of lovely hair just as it is sets it all off to perfection while the way you had it scraped back didn't do much for you at all?'

Sidonie's eyes almost fell out. 'You're joking!'

He grimaced. 'I'm not. It may not be what you see on the pages of *Vogue*, although if you didn't bite your nails that could help, but it's a big improvement on Sidonie Hill as you normally present her to the world.'

'But . . . but there's the rest of me.'

His lips twisted. 'I can't see a great deal wrong with the rest of you either,' he replied prosaically.

'Well, I'm not terribly well-endowed if you must know.'

'That could be a matter of opinion,' he commented. 'You actually have a rather coltish grace.'

'I...I don't know whether I should believe you,' Sidonie said, her brow furrowed in a mighty frown.

He shrugged and looked amused. 'Why don't you test it out, then?'

'How?'

'Just leave your hair the way it is, for starters. Try not to be too serious when you're around boys—it might help to sound a little less learned—I've already mentioned your clothes, and if you could relax, who knows?' He turned away and reached for the oil.

Sidonie stared at his back and was possessed of the strangest impulse, which manifested itself in what she said. 'At twenty-three aren't I bit grown-up for boys?'

'You look about sixteen at the moment,' he said drily.

She bit her lip. 'Well...but the problem of being too serious and learned-sounding—might that not appeal to older men?'

He turned back and looked more amused. 'Once again, who knows?'

'How old are you, Mike?' The words were out before she could stop them and once out the implication was deafening and she blushed vividly but being Sidonie immediately attempted some rationalisation. 'I mean, as an older man yourself, do you find me boring and too learned? I just thought it might give me some sort of guide. However else it may have sounded,' she said lamely, and not entirely honestly, she realised.

The amusement left his eyes; she saw it go and flinched inwardly. Yet he said normally, even whimsically, 'Definitely an older man; I'm thirty-six...' he paused '...and too old for you, friend Sid.' But he held her grey gaze in a level look for a moment before gently prising the knife out of her fingers and briskly slicing the last potato into chips.

She took a breath then said with all the hauteur she could muster, 'That could be a matter of opinion too—speaking purely academically.'

He was unmoved. 'So it could. Speaking generally as well, but not in this case.'

She couldn't help the slightly crestfallen look that came to her eyes but if he noted it he made no comment as he put the chips in the hot oil.

And all she could think of to say was, 'I see.' But then she leant her chin on her hands thoughtfully, looking genuinely puzzled, and said, 'If I were to assure you I had no designs on you at all—which shouldn't be that hard to believe after the way I carried on a few days ago—could we continue this discussion on an academic level?'

An unwilling smile twisted his lips and he murmured, 'The mind boggles but I have no doubt you're going to pursue it to the death so I guess I have little choice. What is it you'd like to know, Miss Hill?'

She tried to marshal her thoughts into order as her father had always trained her to do when confronting a scientific problem and said at last, 'Well. If as you said I'm not quite the rather ordinary, plain person I took myself for, does it mean you have a preference for tall, statuesque brunettes?'

'Not necessarily. It merely means, and you should understand this, Sid——' he glinted a blue glance at her '—that there has to be a certain kind of chemistry between a man and a woman that's a subtle, mysterious thing and is the reason why a man will fall in love with one girl and not ten others who may be equally as beautiful if not more so. And vice versa.' He laid the fillets of sweetlip carefully into the pan.

Sidonie grimaced. Then she said carefully, 'Point taken. On the other hand it crossed my mind to wonder if there wasn't more to it in your case. And by that I mean, on the scale of averages, most men of your age are either married or have been married.'

'True,' he conceded, quite unperturbed. 'But I can assure *you* that I'm perfectly normal.'

Sidonie's lips parted and her eyes widened. 'Oh, I didn't mean *that*,' she said flusteredly. 'I was thinking more along the lines of some deep unhappiness associated with falling in love that had come your way.'

'Sidonie...' he stopped what he was doing to look levelly across at her '...*that* is the kind of daydream impressionable sixteen-year-old girls are notorious for indulging in.'

A wave of colour stained her cheeks as their gazes held and for one horrifying moment she wondered if he was right. Then her natural obstinacy reasserted itself, although obliquely, and she shrugged her slim shoulders gently and said wryly, 'Oh, well, I've told you all about me, I thought you might like to tell me a bit about you, that's all. But naturally I'll respect your wish for privacy. Would you like me to do the salad?'

For a moment he returned her innocent gaze then he muttered inaudibly beneath his breath and said, 'No. Come and watch the fish and observe the temperature I'm cooking the chips at, but promise me one thing—you won't ever attempt to cook chips on your own. That way you could burn the boat down.'

The fish was delicious but dinner was a slightly strained affair until Sidonie said, 'I'm sorry, Mike.'

He lifted an eyebrow at her and looked sceptical.

'No, I am. Could I explain to you what really made me so maddeningly inquisitive?'

He sighed. 'Do you have to?'

'I think so. I don't like to think we're not friends now so I've turned it all over in my mind and decided it's probably only human nature of the feminine variety to feel a bit piqued when you receive a compliment such as you gave me but nevertheless delivered in such a completely disinterested as well as *uninterested* way.'

'I see,' he said gravely.

'But my ego has recovered, I——'

'Do assure me,' he broke in solemnly but she could see the glint of laughter in his eyes.

'Yes.' And she smiled wonderfully at him with both relief and gratitude in her eyes. 'Can we be friends again?'

'I don't see why not.'

They remained friends for about a day and a half but it was a growing cause of concern for Sidonie that, while what she'd told him about feeling piqued was undoubtedly true, what she'd told him about her ego being recovered was not. Added to this she became more and more curious about him and vaguely aware that there was a lot to Mike Brennan that absolutely intrigued her and reinforced her feeling that there might be some mystery about him too. Because, although he was mostly an easy person to live with, there were times when she got the feeling that he withdrew totally. And there were times when she watched him handle the boat or the sails and knew not only that he was a master mariner but kept feeling there had to be more to him ... Why? she wondered several times. And answered herself, Well, perhaps it is because he's such a master mariner yet it's in a very educated way; he's so scientific about the weather and navigation and a lot of other things—maybe he was in the navy once? Then one afternoon she saw him watch a plane fly over them towards Hamilton Island, and got the strangest feeling he knew all about it too.

So it was safe to say she became quite puzzled and concerned, and finally in a way that hit her rather like a sledgehammer despite making him even angrier, if anything, than he'd been over her failed dinner.

CHAPTER THREE

I⊤ STARTED out a beautiful day and they had a glorious sail and then about mid-afternoon dropped
anchor for the night at Nara Inlet, a long finger of
turquoise water surrounded by the steep, tree-clad
cliffs of Hook Island and echoing with birdsong.

'We can do one of two things,' Mike Brennan said.
'Go ashore—there's a good walk and some Aboriginal
cave paintings—or we can have a swim.'

Sidonie's eyes lit up. 'Why don't we do both?'

'You're very energetic, Sid,' he said, glinting her a
lazy smile.

'I love exploring.'

'I might have known. OK, get some exploring gear
on. We'll swim when we get back.'

The walk was wonderful, although steep and rock-
strewn. Sidonie wore one of her two pairs of shorts,
navy blue, with one of her new T-shirts, bright yellow,
and her hair bundled into her floppy white hat. As a
precaution, Mike insisted she smother herself with
insect repellent although he didn't bother himself, and
after they'd landed he found her a sturdy stick just
in case of snakes.

'I feel like—Dr Livingstone,' she confided.

'Then I suppose I'm Mr Stanley.'

She looked him up and down; he had on khaki
shorts, old sandshoes, a much washed khaki shirt and
his red bandanna. 'You look much more like the

descendant of an Apache chief; however, lead on, Mr Stanley, sir!'

He did, with a lightning grin—and was able to demonstrate quite an amazing knowledge of the local flora; he pointed out to her Hoop pines, Pandanus palms and much more as they climbed steadily. And every now and then as the path strayed towards the edge of the cliff they got a bird's-eye view of *Morning Mist* anchored in the waters below.

They had a break at the cave with the Aboriginal paintings and Sidonie was entranced. It was more an overhang of rock than a cave, fenced off and with a boardwalk erected. It was cool and dim beneath the rock and as she stared at each little image scratched into the surface and faintly coloured with pigments made from berries and the earth she got a feeling of timelessness that stayed with her for the rest of the walk.

'You're quiet, Sid,' he said when they stopped in the rocky bed of a dried-up waterfall.

She looked around at the hot, silent bush and said intensely, 'I'm *feeling*. And I think it's an experience I'll treasure forever.'

He squatted down and rinsed his hands in one of the few pools of water left. 'Want to share it?'

She sat down on a smooth boulder. 'This land is so old, isn't it? That's what I'm feeling, an ancient, timeless sort of...looking back. This is the kind of place that really steeps you in it—do you feel that?'

He took a moment to reply, then, 'I couldn't have put it better myself; yes, I do. It happens to me every time I come here.'

'I'm so glad,' she said simply. 'It makes it even more—significant—oh!' She jumped as a sulphur-crested cockatoo erupted out of a tree, squawking stridently.

Mike Brennan laughed and held down his hand to her. 'Noisy devils, aren't they? I think we've come as far as we can go—shall we get back for that swim?'

Back in her cabin, Sidonie considered two things— the fact that she couldn't swim properly and the fact that this was the occasion she'd purchased not one but two bikinis for. She'd been turning over in her mind for the last couple of days whether to tell him about her lack of aquatic ability in case the need should ever arise but had balked at the thought of exposing yet another deficiency. She had hoped that the gentle few strokes of dog paddle she was capable of would take care of all such cooling-off occasions as might arise.

It now struck her that it wasn't that simple off the back of a yacht and this was demonstrated further as the boat rocked and water splashed, indicating that Mike had just dived into the lovely waters of Nara Inlet.

She swallowed then stood up determinedly. She was hot and dusty but faint heart had never won anything and she donned the red bikini, glanced at herself briefly, raised a surprised eyebrow because she didn't look too bad, and went aloft.

All that was to be seen of Mike was a dark head bobbing in the water some distance away and she thought, Good, I can get this over and done with before he comes back. So she climbed down the metal stern ladder that was riveted to the boat, discovered herself still a foot above the water, hesitated poised with one foot and one hand off the ladder, but the decision was taken literally out of her hands as a powerful dinghy shot past, throwing up a wake that rocked *Morning Mist* and caused her out of surprise to lose her single hand-hold and topple into the water.

I don't believe this but I'm drowning, was the next coherent thought that came to her as she entered a green-filtered world, rose to the surface once, choking and coughing, only to sink again with the awful feeling that the water was actually pressing her down and she'd never see the light of day again. But only moments later, although her lungs felt like bursting, a pair of strong arms gathered her up and she and Mike Brennan broke the surface together.

'You idiot,' he yelled right into her ear, 'what the hell are you doing? *Trying* to drown yourself?'

She coughed and retched. 'No. But I can't swim...' And she slumped against him.

She had vague recollections after that of him slinging her over his shoulder in a fireman's grip, somehow climbing the ladder with her and depositing her on the deck then bending over her and applying mouth-to-mouth resuscitation.

'I'm fine,' she said groggily after a few minutes. 'I don't think I swallowed any. Thank you very much——'

'You blasted, bloody little *fool*,' he broke in, sitting back on his heels. 'Why didn't you tell me you couldn't swim?'

'I can swim a bit——'

'For that matter, why did you ever come on a trip like this, let alone ever set foot on a yacht, if you can't swim?'

She sat up and rubbed her hair out of her face. 'Lots of people do that. I read somewhere about an Americas Cup skipper who couldn't swim——'

'Forget him,' he said savagely. 'Who was the idiot who taught you to sail but not to swim?'

Sidonie swallowed. 'My father.'

'So that's where you get it all from!' He glared at her.

'Some of it,' she conceded miserably. 'He wasn't a very practical person. But you see, back home, it's invariably too cold to swim anyway and I always wore a life jacket when I was sailing——'

Mike Brennan swore comprehensively and at length and all on the subject of her, until, although with tears in her eyes, she could take it no longer.

She said, when there was a break, 'Anyway, Mr Brennan, it's probably not a lot of help to one to be able to swim, if you're ditched in the middle of the Pacific. As for your theory about only swimmers setting foot aboard boats, have you considered that *everyone* who boards a plane can't fly?'

There was a taut, crackling silence and for a terrified moment she thought he was going to strike her, such was the anger in his eyes. And in her fright the tears overflowed and she whispered desperately, 'I'm sorry...' and started to shake.

Mike Brennan compressed his mouth into a hard line then swore again, but much less virulently, and he stood up in one lithe movement and picked her up in his arms.

Two minutes later he had her down in the main cabin; he'd wrapped her in a big towel and was sitting with her in his lap with his arms around her. 'It's all right,' he said quietly. 'You didn't drown but you gave me an awful fright because I thought you had.'

'I feel such a fool,' she said through chattering teeth.

'Well, I can't say its entirely unwarranted—to simply plunge off the boat like that was taking a huge risk, but——'

'I didn't do it quite like that.'

'Sidonie,' he warned.

'No, please let me tell you. All I was hoping to do was dip myself in and hold on to the bottom rung of the ladder if I could but when that dinghy came past I lost my grip and fell, you see.'

She felt a jolt of laughter beneath her cheek as it lay on his chest. He also said, 'You aren't exactly endowed with luck either, are you?'

'Not a lot.' And she began to shake again.

He grimaced above her head and gathered her closer, and said nothing for about five minutes until the spasm passed. Then he said, 'How would it be if I made us some really exotic cocktails like Mai Tais and we took them up on deck and saluted the sunset over this ancient, timeless place? Do you think you're up to that?'

Sidonie moved her cheek against his chest, closed her eyes and was hit by the knowledge that she could die quite easily for Mike Brennan, that she'd passed from liking him to loving him, that she'd be content to experience the lovely feeling of being in his arms forever, that he thrilled her in way she'd never been thrilled before just to watch him move and to feel his strength—and all this without knowing a thing about him other than that, for her, he was all she needed to feel happy and safe.

Her lashes fluttered then she sat up abruptly and launched into speech. 'One good thing about me, despite my horrific luck, is that I always bounce back. I'd love that. I'll just put a shirt on.'

But he held her back with his hands about her waist. 'Sure?' he queried. 'I mean that you're feeling OK now.'

'Yes, I'm sure,' she said huskily but gathered the towel closer in case he could see the way her heart was beating beneath her bikini-top.

He let her go but with a faint frown in his eyes and she climbed off his lap. He said after a moment, 'Meet you on the bridge in a few minutes, then, First Mate Hill.'

'Aye, aye, skipper!' And she sketched a salute.

She put her other new T-shirt on, brushed her hair, stared into her eyes in the mirror, observed the slightly stunned look in them and turned away to take several deep breaths.

The Mai Tais were delicious, the sunset spectacular and their conversation desultory and mainly concerned with the other boats arriving in Nara to anchor for the night. Then Mike's eyes narrowed as a sleek fly-bridge cruiser with *Moonshine* painted on it in big bold letters nosed past them and several persons could be seen waving energetically.

'Hell,' he said, waving back.

'Friends of yours?' Sidonie enquired.

'Mmm. Very noisy, excitable and social friends. I was hoping to avoid them.'

'They must be strange friends if you'd rather avoid them,' she commented.

'Oh——' he looked wry '—at the right time and place they're OK. You'll no doubt meet them tomorrow.'

'You don't have to include me.'

'All the same I'm going to. There's only one way to deal with Tim Molloy and that's get it over and done with. I'll ask them over for a barbecue lunch. That might just stave off being invaded by them to-night. You don't look up to that.'

'I'm fine really but——' Sidonie looked doubtful and realised at the same moment that she was bone-weary.

'I thought so,' he murmured, getting up. 'I'll radio them and tell them we aren't receiving visitors.'

Sidonie felt herself colour. 'Could you...not tell them why?'

He smiled briefly. 'It'll be our secret. I'm only sur-prised you haven't asked me to teach you to swim, though.' A wicked little glint lit his eyes.

'Could you?' Her eyes widened.

'I expect I could have a go. It might take a bit of a load off my mind. Now, a light meal and bed for you, my dear, and no arguments.'

'Can I make the salad?'

'Be my guest,' Mike Brennan said as he laid out steaks, sausages and chops on a platter.

'Could you also tell me a bit more about these people?' Sidonie settled herself on her stool with the chopping-board in front of her and a selection of salad items: tomatoes, a mignonette lettuce, a green cap-sicum, cucumber, snow peas, shallots and a punnet of beansprouts. She'd also selected a large, clear Guzzini bowl to put the results of her labours into.

Not only was *Morning Mist* fitted out elegantly but the crockery and cutlery and even the plastic ware was of the highest quality. She paused for a moment and considered that whoever owned the boat not only had good taste but a lot of money.

'Tim Malloy is an orthodontist who's made a small fortune out of teeth. His other great love, if anyone could love other people's teeth, is boating. He will have his current girlfriend with him, having split up with his wife. The other couple on board are not that well-known to me but Tim loves to be surrounded by a crowd.'

'I see,' Sidonie said and frowned.

'What's exercising your mind now, friend Sid?' Mike Brennan enquired.

'Well, they sound like ... party people,' she mused. 'I'm not very good in that kind of company generally.'

'It's never wise to prejudge people, Sidonie,' he replied thoughtfully.

'Oh, I agree with you entirely!' She waved the chopping-knife but grimaced. 'It's just that I've had a few—um—unfortunate experiences, you might say.' She went back to slicing cucumber.

'Such as?'

'Well, I'm not good at making conversation, idle conversation——'

'That's funny—you never stop talking to me.'

'That's different! And I often don't understand jokes or the kind of banter that goes on and I find myself straining every nerve to join in, *knowing* I must seem like a wet blanket, and it all, for some strange reason, actually affects my hearing.'

'Good God!' Mike Brennan grinned. 'Why?'

'I don't know,' she said gloomily and reached for the capsicum. 'Plus, now,' she added, 'I'm more conscious than ever that I come over as too "learned".'

'For which you lay the blame squarely at my feet?'

Sidonie raised a troubled grey gaze to his. 'Not for the actual fact of it, of course, just making me . . . feel it more acutely.'

He studied her in silence for a long moment. Then his lips twitched and he said, 'I was wrong.'

Sidonie blinked. 'Wrong?'

'To tell you to try to change yourself. To make you feel uncomfortable with yourself. The only thing I wasn't wrong about was that it would help to relax a bit.'

Her lips parted. 'I don't understand . . .'

'It's quite simple.' For some reason he smiled a dry little smile. 'You're unique just as you are. And some day the *right* bloke will understand that and appreciate it and probably never let you get away from him. I hear,' he said, looking up, 'our guests approaching.'

Sidonie closed her mouth with a click and was galvanised into action. Then she looked down at herself despairingly, at her white shorts and old T-shirt. 'I haven't even changed!'

He laughed and came round the island counter to take her chin lightly in his fingers. 'So many worries. If I know this mob, they'll be wearing next to nothing so just pop your red bikini on and you'll be fine.'

She hesitated. 'I've got another one—not associated so far with all but drowning.'

He lifted a lazy eyebrow. 'I didn't figure you for a two-bikini girl somehow, Sid.'

'I wasn't. I bought *both* of them in a rush of blood the day we met at Airlie Beach.'

'Then you definitely shouldn't waste them,' he said gravely.

Despite her fears, the barbecue was going well and she was actually enjoying herself when it happened.

Mike had rigged up a canvas awning over the aft deck and the barbecue itself was attached to the stern rail so it was sitting mainly over water and a convenient breeze was wafting the smoke away from them. Tim Molloy was a giant of a man with curly red hair but with a persistent, all-embracing kind of friendliness that was hard to resist. His current girlfriend was a languid brunette with a stunning figure but she too was friendly and the other couple the same. They had brought with them several bottles of champagne and before long the kind of friendly banter Sidonie normally found hard to cope with was going on, but, and perhaps it was to do with drinking champagne at eleven o'clock in the morning, while she didn't suddenly find herself becoming the life and soul of the party, she didn't feel a freak either.

It might even be to do with the fact that I'm dressed right for once, she mused. She'd put on her hyacinth floral bikini with a plain blue blouse on top but unbuttoned. Both the other girls were wearing bikinis as Mike had predicted. She'd also left her hair loose—and hadn't known whether to be amused or otherwise when Tim Molloy had taken her hand in his large paw upon being introduced, and said with a genuine glint of admiration in his eyes, 'Well, now, I see Mike hasn't lost his talent for choosing attractive crew!'

Mike Brennan had grimaced as Sidonie had opened her mouth but she'd shut it upon reflection and merely murmured something incomprehensible with a faint blush.

They'd all inspected the boat eagerly from bow to stern and come to the conclusion that she was a beauty. 'The best yet, I'd say, Mike, old son.' Tim had clapped him heartily on the shoulder. 'Where will you stop?'

Mike had shrugged. 'Who knows?' And shot Tim an oddly penetrating look, Sidonie thought. Which had led her to think further that here was someone who knew Mike Brennan, knew his background and that she might just glean some information on the subject.

She didn't, at least not a lot other than the fact that they were all, bar her, a cosmopolitan, sophisticated group of people who could discuss the latest news on the EC, the appalling sales tax on foreign luxury cars, whether the state Labour government of Victoria would be re-elected, as well as this divine restaurant in Sydney or, in the case of the girls, the latest state of the boutique on Hamilton Island and what they might wear to the Melbourne Cup.

Curiously, or perhaps not so—she had decided he wasn't a rough diamond after all—Mike seemed to be quite at home in all this talk. Not that he was as loquacious as his friend Tim Molloy but it was obvious that they had friends in common and that Mike was entirely abreast not only of world affairs but social-page affairs. It was also obvious that both girls were impressed by him.

Yet he wore his faded khaki shirt, his red bandanna, a pair of entirely nondescript white shorts that looked as if they could have got mixed up with some un-colourfast colours in a washing machine and sported none of the gold chains or Rolex Oyster watches the other two men wore with Benetton T-shirts and expensively colourful togs. It's his body, Sidonie thought with a curious little pang, so tall and strong but with not an ounce of surplus flesh, and that red Indian face you can't *read*, and those deep blue eyes that are capable of looking so amused yet give nothing else away—and she took a despairing sip of champagne.

Which was when it happened. Karen, Tim's girl-friend, moved herself out of the shade and casually took off her bikini-top. Then she leant back against a stanchion, closed her eyes and offered herself and her voluptuously beautiful figure to the sun. No one appeared to take the slightest bit of notice bar Sidonie, who choked on a sip of champagne, choked again when the other girl followed suit as if it was the most natural thing in the world, and fled down the ladder mumbling something about getting the salad.

Mike followed her down and it was not hard to see the quizzical look in his eyes as she stood in the middle of the cabin with her hands pressed to her cheeks. 'A problem, Sid?' he murmured.

She took her hands away. 'Of *course*. I feel as if I've strayed into a nudist colony!'

'I take it you don't approve of that kind of thing?'

'No, I don't! Do you?'

He shrugged. 'It happens quite a lot in this part of the world——'

'That could be a justification for just about any-thing—rape, murder, heaven knows what.'

'If you let me finish, it's *not* a prelude to an orgy in this case, simply an expression of freedom—or something to that effect—on their part. They even have a bare-breasted race day during the Hamilton Island fun-race week, which is only a couple of weeks away as a matter of fact.'

Sidonie stared up at him. 'They may well have,' she said tartly, 'but if you're expecting *me* to——'

'Perish the thought,' he said seriously. 'It never crossed my mind.'

'So I should hope,' she said crossly. 'But you sound as if you approve of it all!' she added even more crossly.

'As a matter of fact I don't——'

'Well, I didn't see you ordering them to cover up!'

He grimaced wryly. 'No. What I meant was, I personally don't find it any sort of a turn-on. However, it's quite possible that's not the spirit it was intended in anyway.'

For once in her life, Sidonie expressed an extremely cynical sentiment. 'Want to bet?'

He stared at her, his lips twitching until she coloured hotly and had to look away and say exasperatedly, 'Why do I get the feeling I'm being prudish in the extreme? *Is* it so...whatever, to be shocked and embarrassed?'

He watched her thoughtfully for a moment then said with a lift of an eyebrow, 'No. Not for someone like you. But it's a pity to let it spoil your day; I got the impression you were enjoying yourself.'

'I was...'

'Then why don't you look on it as simply enlarging your experience of life? You could still maintain your internal disapproval if you wanted to—I don't think you'd be seriously compromising your ethics or yourself.'

'Well, I suppose I could try,' she said reluctantly.

'That wasn't so bad, was it?' Mike remarked a few hours later as they waved his guests off.

'No,' Sidonie said consideringly.

He glinted a faint smile in her direction. 'You and Karen even had a heart-to-heart chat,' he murmured.

Sidonie bit her lip. 'I may have misjudged Karen, in that I think she is one of those freedom-loving persons as opposed to being—what I thought she was.'

'Also not thick,' he commented. 'She obviously felt your disapproval and clothed herself accordingly.'

This was true. By the time Sidonie had returned to the deck after her outburst to Mike, both girls had put their tops back on and, although they'd made absolutely nothing of it, Sidonie, if anything, had felt worse. She sighed dispiritedly. 'I told you I was a bit of a social disaster.'

'No, you're not, my friend Sid,' he replied bracingly but with that wicked glint in his eye she was coming to know well, 'just a nice kid, that's all. And before you take issue with that I'm taking the dinghy to collect my crab pots and the tide is right for a bit of oyster-gathering. How would it be if I showed you how to make oyster mornay this evening?'

She brightened. 'Lovely. I'll clean up in the meantime.'

It gave her an odd sense of satisfaction to clear away the remains of the barbecue and restore *Morning Mist* to perfection. Indeed, when she'd finished, she made herself a cup of tea and curled up on the settee with it and looked around. It's like home, she thought with a pang. It's more like a home to me than I've ever known, what's worse, and that's not just because it's a lovely, comfortable boat but...

She swallowed and could no longer put off coming to grips with what she felt about Mike Brennan. But, to her intense desolation, nothing she tried to tell herself about it being out of the question to fall in love with a man you barely knew seemed to make the slightest dent in the fact that she had.

She smiled sadly and thought of the French phrase *coup de foudre*, the stroke of lightning, and thought, So it is possible to be hit by love in this manner; *they* know, not that it helps me in the slightest. Only this morning he made it quite plain he wasn't the right man for me. I wish I knew why... Well, it's obvious why; he simply doesn't return the emotion, but why do I get the feeling, *still*, that there's some mystery about him? Because, she answered herself, it just doesn't seem to fit that a man like Mike does nothing more in life than skipper yachts for other people.

She stared into space for a long moment then got up with a helpless little shrug and decided to shower and change. And it was hard to admit what prompted her to do it, particularly in light of the things she'd said, but some impulse stopped her on the way to her cabin, turned her in the direction of Mike's, which she happened to know, because she'd cleaned it in her bid to restore the boat after filling it with greasy black smoke, had a full-length mirror behind the door.

She also told herself she was quite safe as she stared at her image in it, because she would hear the dinghy returning, and she took off her blouse then unhooked her bikini-top and let it fall to the floor. But no sooner was the deed done than she felt the boat rock, heard someone coming down the ladder and gasped in sheer horror as he opened the cabin door and discovered her half naked in it.

'Oh, no!' she said, distraught, and scrabbled for her blouse.

'Why, Sidonie,' he said abruptly after stopping short, 'this is a surprise.'

Her face, her whole body now barely concealed by her bunched-up blouse held in her hands, felt scorched with shame. 'I didn't *hear* you. I——'

He smiled briefly. 'I ran out of fuel so I had to row. And the keys for the locker with the outboard fuel in it are in here.' He nodded to the table beside the double bed.

'Oh,' she said hollowly. 'W-well, I suppose you'd like some sort of an explanation.'

His lips twisted. 'Only if you want to; it's not exactly a crime.'

'I don't *really* want to, except to say I had no intention of...I only have a small mirror in my bathroom and...if you must know...' she sighed unhappily and her shoulders slumped '...I was possessed of an impulse to see how *I* looked without my top. I know that must sound crazy to you after the things I said—I don't know what got into me,' she finished miserably and studied her feet, wishing she could just disappear through the floor.

'And?'

Her lashes fluttered up. 'I...I don't know what you mean,' she stammered.

'What was the verdict?'

'I didn't get much of a chance to form any verdict other than that, as I always knew, I'm not particularly well-endowed. Beside Karen I—there doesn't seem to be any contest.'

Mike Brennan shook his head and there was something very wry and amused as well as oddly gentle in his eyes as he said, 'I told you once before, that could be a matter of opinion. In fact if you want the opinion of a—rather old campaigner, you have a delicate, rose-tinted little figure that would be a delight to many a beholder. So cheer up, Sid. Quantity and quality are never the same thing. Would you mind if I got those keys now? It's getting dark and I want to fill up the outboard and winch the dinghy up so we can make an early start tomorrow. If you'd also like to start grating some cheese, I'll shortly commence my cooking lesson for the day.'

'Is that enough?'

Mike glanced at the mound of grated cheese. 'Plenty. We'll put most of it in the sauce and reserve a little for sprinkling on top, and we pour the sauce over the oysters and pop them under the grill.'

'White sauce,' Sidonie mused, 'brings back memories I'd prefer to forget.'

He grimaced. 'Well, come round and see exactly how it's done. Here.' He handed her a wooden spoon. 'Just stir it gently and consistently. As you'll observe, it's cooking over a very low flame.'

Sidonie stirred intently for a few minutes with the appearance of absolute concentration. But the fact of the matter was her concentration was divided because she couldn't get out of her mind what he'd said earlier—about her having a delicate, rose-tinted figure that would be a delight to many a beholder... And just to think of it made her feel curiously tremulous yet strangely sad. Indeed, her hand trembled on the spoon and she had to clench her teeth to settle herself down.

That was when she heard Mike laugh softly and say, 'Relax, kid, cooking's not really such a desperate occupation. Once you appreciate the cause and effects of it as you so obviously do in anything mechanical, it'll be a breeze.'

She made a deliberate effort to relax. 'Sorry, I was thinking of something else actually——' She broke off and bit her lip.

He looked at her with his lips twisting. 'I hesitate to ask this but—it's not to do with anything else you haven't told me, is it?'

She blinked.

'Like not being able to swim,' he said gently.

'Oh. Oh, no! I really don't think I have any secrets from you now,' she said, realised the terrible untruth of it as the words left her mouth and started to stir extremely agitatedly.

'Sid——' his hand closed over hers on the spoon '—I don't think we need another disaster associated with white sauce—what's the matter?'

She stared at his lean brown hand over hers and was struck by a sensation of pure sensuality for the first time in her life. But it wasn't just the feel of his hand on hers, it was the total, overwhelming consciousness of him so close to her, the clean yet purely male tang of him, the desire to rest against him and be held, to bury herself in his arms and be a part of him, to wonder, if she offered him her rose-tinted body, whether she could afford him some respite from whatever burdens he carried, because she was sure there were some, or simply to bring him a little pleasure.

'N-nothing,' she said unsteadily, but with herculean effort managed to sigh lightly then. 'I guess it's been an unsettling day,' she said musingly. 'I've sort of had to rethink some of my convictions; I put myself in a position which left me feeling really silly. I . . . well, that's about it in a nutshell.'

'Then perhaps I ought to finish this,' he murmured with nothing more than one fleeting but unfairly acute glance into her eyes. 'Tell you what, take a break from being taught for tonight and why don't you plot a course for tomorrow instead? I thought we might go to Border Island but we'll need the wind and the tide right.'

'Oh!' Despite herself Sidonie brightened. 'I'd love to. What's at Border?' She released the spoon and he released her hand and she moved round the island bench smoothly, she hoped.

'Wonderful coral and a great view from the saddle of the island. Then I thought we might make our way down to Whitehaven Beach for a night, do Gulnare Inlet, which should really appeal to your exploring instincts—it's been likened to travelling up the Limpopo—perhaps Cid Harbour, and then Hamilton. I think . . .' he paused '. . . that's a fairly comprehensive tour of the Whitsundays.'

Before she stopped to think Sidonie said, 'But what about Butterfly Bay and Blue Pearl Bay? And Haslewood Island, and Macona——'

'We could find ourselves in any of those, Sid, depending on the wind, apart from Blue Pearl and Butterfly, but doing the lot could see us running out of time,' he replied tranquilly.

'Oh!' She thought for a moment and discovered a thread of anxiety running through her mind that she couldn't at first identify. Then it came to her—was this a subtle way of telling her the trip had to end? Was it even a subtle way of warning her it might end sooner than planned? Why? Because he knows, she thought, what I'm going through? Please, God, no...

But she swallowed and knew in her bones she was right—and practised a kind of deliberate deceit that came so naturally it secretly astounded her. But the plain fact was that she couldn't bear to contemplate the day it would end even if it meant hiding better all she felt for him, so she said with a grin, 'You're the skipper! Whatever you say goes,' and turned away to the chart table.

She didn't see the way he studied her back with a faint frown in his eyes for a moment before he turned back to the white sauce.

CHAPTER FOUR

THE view, as Mike had predicted, was wonderful from Border Island. To the west lay the bulk of Hook and Whitsunday Islands, to the south, Haslewood, and to the east Deloraine Island shimmering in the sunlight yet looking mysterious and aloof, and, beyond, the great expanse of the Coral Sea to the horizon. There were, Sidonie knew from all she'd read now, great coral reefs between her and the horizon like a huge barrier to the might of the Pacific, which was how they'd got their collective name, the Great Barrier Reef, and she longed to sail out to them but Mike didn't mention it and she, following her new policy, didn't suggest it.

She thought about her 'new policy' as she sat on top of the saddle on Border Island and fanned herself with her hat. Non-interventionist? Non-aligned—no, that wasn't the right term either but non-something. Well, to be as unrevealing as she could. To simply be a friendly, competent crewperson. Not, she reflected, that she'd had much chance to implement this policy as yet—one morning. But as they'd sailed towards Border, across a deep inky blue sea with a white froth below the bow and in their wake, she'd been just that. And in the exhilaration of a fifteen-knot breeze it hadn't been hard; the way *Morning Mist* had sliced through the water had thrilled them both.

No, she reflected, the hard times are still to come. Perhaps if I can keep busy...

'Ready to go back, Miss Livingstone? If we leave it any longer we'll have to carry the dinghy over the coral.'

She jumped up. 'I hadn't thought of that!'

'The tide, up here, waits for no man. As it is we'll have to slog through some mud.'

But Sidonie actually found that fascinating too. She kept stopping to inspect shells; she delighted in the clams that closed their fleshy, brilliantly hued lips—emerald and black-striped, vermilion, purple—and spurted a stream of water upwards if they really felt threatened, and she shuddered at some of the less delicate coral that when exposed above the water was fleshy and slimy and altogether repellent.

But her faith was restored once in the dinghy when they did a tour of the reef surrounding Border and had a marvellous view of the better coral.

'I'm glad,' Mike remarked when she told him this. 'Such enthusiasm deserves to be rewarded.'

'All the same it's good to have a good shudder now and then!'

'I noticed,' he said ruefully, his eyes resting on her glowing face.

Sidonie grimaced. 'I suppose you've seen it so many times it doesn't affect you greatly now.'

'I wouldn't say that,' he reflected wryly. 'I just don't think I've ever seen it with anyone who has appreciated it all quite as much as you do.'

It was like a treasure, a gold nugget to hug to herself, even this wry approval—But, remember, she warned herself immediately, don't make too much of it. So she said, 'Would you like me to service the outboard this afternoon?' She patted the cowling of the motor.

'It and the dinghy are about the only things I've noticed about *Morning Mist* that aren't new.'

He looked at her. 'There's not a great deal of the afternoon left.'

'If that's a way of saying you wouldn't trust me to do it——'

'It's not, but——'

'You never know, I might be able to coax a half-knot more out of it. How long since it was last serviced?'

He lifted an eyebrow. 'You're going to love this, Sid; I have no idea. I . . . there was a new one ordered but it didn't arrive on time so I had to make do with this one, which was second-hand.'

'There you are, you see. I just knew it was crying out for some attention,' she said triumphantly.

'OK, OK!' He brought the dinghy up to the stern of the boat. 'Go ahead.'

She did just that.

She changed into her cut-off overalls and laid a canvas sheet on the aft deck upon which Mike placed the motor. She assembled her tools and said seriously, 'Please feel free to do anything you like; this will keep me busy for an hour or two.'

'Why, thank you,' he replied gravely.

She bit her lip. 'I didn't mean it to sound like that.'

'Sound like what?'

'As if I was trying to get rid of you.'

'That never crossed my mind,' he marvelled.

'I'd be glad if I thought I could believe you but——'

'And I can't help wondering why you're trying to get rid of me, Sid.'

She cast him a look of exasperation. 'Well, I thought you might *like* not to have me talking the hind leg off a donkey at you. Actually. As well as me earning my keep.'

He rose from his squatting position and ruffled her hair in a supremely avuncular gesture. 'I'm going.' But he was laughing at her, she knew, and she just prayed that it wasn't because he'd seen through her machinations. Which wasn't a very nice thing to do, she thought rebelliously, then sighed, and commanded herself simply to concentrate on the task at hand.

So she took the outboard motor apart and checked for any loose or damaged parts. Then she lubricated the gear housing and checked the oil level, serviced the spark plug, cleaned the fuel filters and removed a bit of gunk from the fuel cap air vent. Finally she checked the anode and decided it had a bit of life in it yet. Then she reassembled it all and by the time she was finished there was barely enough light to see by and she stood up and stretched and yawned.

'All done?' Mike said behind her. He'd left her strictly alone until now and all she'd heard of him was when he'd made a sea-phone call.

'Mmm. It's not in bad condition although you'll need a new anode shortly and there are a couple of nicks and rust patches on the propeller that should be attended to, but nothing desperate.' She wiped her hand across her forehead and left a streak of grease there. 'I guarantee it will run just that bit sweeter now, though.'

'I'm sure it will. Why don't you have a shower?' He regarded her quizzically.

'All right, I'll just clear up here——'

'I'll do that; you've earnt your keep well and truly today, First Mate Hill.'

She flushed with pleasure and hoped he didn't notice in the growing twilight. 'Thanks,' she said simply and turned away.

And that was how she kept things for the next couple of days—simple, she thought. I could just as well be a boy first mate—excepting I don't suppose he'd teach a boy to cook . . .

But she had to acknowledge that the weather was a help for those days—breezy but hot and bright— and they did all the things he'd mentioned. They spent a night off Whitehaven Beach, a three-mile expanse of pure white silica sand from a bygone geological age and quite different from most of the Whitsunday beaches that were not that white or fine and degenerated into mudflats when the tide went out, and they walked the full length of it. They sailed round to Cid Harbour, her namesake, she said, since it was pronounced 'Sid', and had a wonderful ramble through the bush to Dugong Beach fringed with casuarinas that made soft music as the breeze sighed through them. And it was all going so well until Gulnare . . .

They spent a night in Gulnare Inlet and the next morning travelled up it by dinghy right to its head. It was a huge, shallow inlet; at first Sidonie said that with its thickly wooded peaks it reminded her of Switzerland without the snow. But of course at eye-level the ever-present mangrove trees dispelled that image, and she decided they were really eerie although clever sort of trees that grew quite happily in salt water.

'It *is* like going up the Limpopo!' was her final decision as the dinghy hummed along and they explored the narrowing waterway near its head.

Mike grinned at her. 'It's not, actually.'

Her interest quickened. 'You've been there? To Africa?'

He shrugged. 'I've seen it. There are crocodiles in it.'

She shivered. 'There could be crocodiles here!'

'I've never heard of any—there are huge mud crabs, however——'

'What were you doing in Africa, Mike?' She looked at him with genuine interest and curiosity in her eyes. 'I would *love* to go there.'

He shrugged. 'A bit of flying.'

Her eyes widened and she nearly fell off her perch on the side of the dinghy in her excitement. 'I knew it!'

'Knew what?'

'That you were a pilot as well.'

'How?'

'You know so much about navigation, celestial and otherwise, and weather patterns et cetera, it just crossed my mind—and the way you watched a plane one day too. I would love to learn to fly,' she said seriously.

He laughed. 'Perhaps you should concentrate on swimming and cooking first.'

She felt instantly demolished and said in a stiff little voice, 'Did someone say that to you when you wanted to learn to fly?'

He grimaced. 'No. But——'

'Then you shouldn't say it to me.'

He eyed her averted profile and kept his face straight. 'My apologies, I shouldn't have. I could say instead that you'd probably take to flying like a duck to water, but as we haven't commenced your swimming lessons yet I'll have to think of another analogy, won't I?'

Sidonie forgot her dignified stance and flashed him a suddenly blazing look. 'Of all the appallingly ped-estrian attempts at male chauvinism I've heard, that has to be the worst!'

'Oh, dear,' he drawled. 'I'm demolished.'

'No, you're not! You're secretly still laughing at me if I know you, Mr Brennan—don't think I can't tell by your eyes!'

'Then I'll have to veil my emotions from my eyes, Sid——'

'Don't bother,' she said bitterly, 'on my account.'

He was silent for a moment as she gazed stonily ahead, then he said, 'What are we really fighting about, Sid?'

'I'm fighting about being treated like a stupid girl.'

'Then I do apologise; perhaps I was a bit thoughtless in the things I said. You're the least stupid girl I know in lots of ways.'

Sidonie thought for a bit. 'Thank you,' she said at last.

His lips twitched. 'It seems to be very important to you not to be lumped in with the rest of the female population.'

She shrugged. 'It's a help to be good at some things, when you're so obviously not much good at others.'

'Such as?'

She bit her lip. 'Well, I guess you know better than most what those are—uh—but I have no intention of getting maudlin on the subject, especially as you've apologised.'

He appeared to contemplate this for a while then he said lightly, 'Could you tell me how to get back into your good graces? I have the feeling a mere apology hasn't done it.'

Don't shut me out... She didn't say it but it was the thought that rose to the surface of her mind immediately and as she examined it she realised that that was probably what had upset her as much as anything else—or was she wrong in imagining that the way he'd teased her had had another side to it? Had been in fact a bid to head her off from trespassing into his flying days? But why wouldn't he want to talk about that? I must have imagined it—and that's a serious blow to your policy, Sidonie, she warned herself...

'Sid?'

'Oh.' She blinked. 'I don't know—I mean you don't, of course. Have to do anything.' She tried to inject some perkiness into her voice. 'You're the boss.' But instead of perky all she sounded was desolate.

'Sid,' he said with no emotion at all as he steered the dinghy round a mangrove tree reaching its green tulip clusters across the water, 'don't fall in love with me.'

She gasped and nearly fell off the dinghy again—and found herself saying hotly as she scrambled back into position, 'I don't know you mean! Why should I do that?'

'Well, as to why not, I'd be a lousy candidate from your point of view,' he replied.

She took a jerky breath. 'All right.'

He lifted an ironic eyebrow at her. 'Just—all right?'

'I don't want to talk about it any more,' she said with some agitation, 'but you're actually quite safe from me, Mike—why does that ring a bell?' she asked more of herself and probably out of sheer nerves.

'Because it's exactly what I said to you one memorable day.'

'So you did—oh, hell,' she said hollowly, swallowed, and took a deep breath. 'Could we just pretend this conversation never arose?'

'We could,' he said drily, 'but——'

'Mike, I don't have to be told things over and over. Please at least grant me that much...of my self-respect,' she said evenly and looked at him steadily for a moment.

'So it was a problem?' he said slowly and totally disregarding her plea.

Sidonie gritted her teeth and sent up a short little prayer for some divine intervention. What to say? 'I,' she began, 'toyed with the idea, yes——'

'Despite what you said earlier?'

'There's an old saying about pride coming before a fall,' she said, thinking carefully. 'It's a very pride-denting experience to be...admonished not to fall in love with someone, as you would know if you'd ever experienced it, so what I said first was said out of pride—do I have to go on?' she added in suddenly goaded tones. 'This is also very embarrassing and why on earth you had to choose this marvellous inlet that I was enjoying so much to...totally—talk about being demolished!—I can't imagine. So yes,' she said baldly, 'it was a problem. It's not any more.' And she turned away resolutely.

He said quietly, 'I'm sorry, Sid.'

She refused to turn back but said gruffly, 'So am I. I guess this wrecks things, though, doesn't it?'

'Nothing will ever wreck some aspects of it. But I think it would be best if I dropped you off at Hamilton tomorrow. You can get back to the mainland easily from there; I'll buy you a ticket.'

'OK.' She licked a salty tear off her lip and dug into the depths of her being for some moral strength. 'I wonder if I could get a job on Hamilton?' She turned back at last, her face earnest beneath her floppy white hat.

'I think . . .' he said slowly, then appeared to change his mind. 'You could always try.'

'Mmm . . . Or perhaps someone else needs crew—no.' She grimaced. 'When they find out I'm so hopeless in the kitchen—no—oh! I think we're at the head. Shall we get off and explore?'

They did but only briefly. Then they drove, nearly all the way in silence, back to *Morning Mist*.

And after getting aboard she stood in the middle of the main cabin for a long moment and looked around. Then she grimaced and gave herself a little shake and once again dug into the depths of her soul as she heard him come down the ladder behind her. 'We haven't checked the motor for a few days. We should, you know,' she said seriously.

'All right.' He looked at her penetratingly. 'We'll do it this afternoon.'

'You know——' Sidonie squatted on her heels and wiped her hands on a rag '—your eutectic refrigeration system puzzles me a bit. I really feel there should be an automatic cut-off switch when it gets to, say, minus twenty degrees. One could quite easily forget to do it manually in certain conditions—if you had to motor for hours, for example—and then you could freeze or burst the pipes.'

'It's a thought,' Mike agreed. 'Tricky things, eutectics.'

'Yes... But otherwise I don't think you have a thing to worry about.' She gave the Gardiner a fond farewell pat and clambered out of the engine-well.

Mike followed her and together they put the covers back. 'I don't know about you,' he said as he straightened, 'but I'd be quite happy to heat up a frozen lasagne tonight—we've been down there for hours.'

Sidonie laughed although she winced inwardly. 'Sorry, I probably got carried away. Yes, that would be fine. I'll go and clean up.' She turned away and hoped he hadn't noticed anything wrong, because the reason she'd winced was on account of the frozen lasagne and what it stood for—no cooking lesson tonight. No companionable time while she sat perched on her stool across the counter from him and chopped or peeled and they enjoyed a glass of wine while he demonstrated how it was done.

She was right, she discovered when she emerged from her cabin, clean and shining. It was all ready—lasagne, a salad and banana fritters for dessert. But she made no comment and tried throughout the meal to be as normal as possible.

It was unfair that there should be a sliver of bright white moon that night, though, because when they took their coffee up to the cockpit, as they'd got into the habit of doing, it was shining over Gulnare Inlet in a way that made her throat close up and made her totally lose the flow of easy chatter she'd maintained.

'What will you do?' Mike said quietly into the silence.

She looked over the silvered water and didn't pretend to misunderstand. 'I haven't altogether decided, but I will go home to Melbourne.'

'Home?'

'Well, it is my home town.'

'When did you make that decision?'

In the shower, a short while ago, she answered in her mind. And why? Because to stay around on Hamilton Island or anywhere up here would be foolish and look as if I haven't given up hope...

'I think it's the sensible decision,' she said. 'I do have some contacts down there—friends of my father and so on.'

She thought she heard him sigh as he said, 'Sid— I'm sorry——'

'That's all right,' she cut in. 'It's not your fault. And it's not even as if I'd got to the stage of picturing myself going to bed with you so I'm certainly not a lost cause or anything like that.' And her voice had been surprisingly steady.

He studied her for a moment. 'Do you have any experience of that?'

'Sleeping with someone?'

'Yes,' he said a shade drily.

'Not actually, no.'

He raised an eyebrow. 'Yet you went out and got yourself a steady boyfriend?'

She looked rueful. 'I know it's not the way things are done these days and I didn't just—go out and get myself a steady boyfriend as you put it. We'd known each other for years. We were at school together then uni.' She stopped and bit her lip.

'All the same, boys or very young men are renowned for their fascination with the opposite sex and their eagerness to experiment,' he said, and waited.

Sidonie rubbed her mouth. 'I suppose it does sound strange,' she said reluctantly and frowned. 'Of course, I've thought about it a lot since it ended—more, possibly, than I did at the time. And you see, I think Peter was as...naïve and lonely as I was. He'd been orphaned when he was about ten and his grandparents brought him up and it was a fairly restricted, old-fashioned sort of upbringing—not that they were *ogres* or anything like that but I'm sure you know what I mean.'

'Yes.'

'So...' she paused '...when everyone around us seemed to be pairing up we decided—I mean, we did everything together—sailed, studied, went to parties—and his grandparents approved of me—well, probably because they sensed I wasn't...much into that,' she said on a lowering note with a sigh. 'Of course I should have realised all this then.'

'What did your father think?'

'He seemed to be happy about it! So long, he said, as we didn't plan to rush into marriage, which we'd actually never even thought about! I wonder why he...?' She frowned.

'I think I can guess,' Mike said with some irony. 'He probably got the same vibes as Peter's grandparents. Be that as it may—didn't you indulge in any of the physical side of love?'

A tinge of colour crept into Sidonie's cheeks. 'Not much,' she confessed with scrupulous honesty, however. 'But we used to hold hands and put our arms around each other and kiss each other goodnight and

it was warm and comfortable and I . . . and I suppose
we thought the rest of it would take care of itself when
the time came,' she finished on a note of something
like defiance.

'I wasn't suggesting otherwise,' he commented.

'Is that absolutely true?' she queried a little tartly.

He smiled briefly. 'If you must know, what you
said represented an innocence that was—rather
touching.'

Sidonie chewed her lip then said bleakly, 'The only
problem, of course, was that while I was cruising along
in my innocence love hit him on the head—bonk! Just
like that.' She gestured expressively with the flat of
her hand.

'And now you feel it's happened to you.'

'Not bonk,' she said with a fleeting grin, but
sobered almost immediately. 'It sort of—grew. Now,
though, I know it's just one of those experiences.
Life's probably full of them—I mean, they feel a bit
agonising at the time but they fade away.'

She felt his hand on the top of her head, very lightly
and only for the barest moment. 'For what it's worth,
Sid, I doubt if the memory of you will ever fade away
completely and I'm not worth much agonising over,
believe me . . . I think we should go to bed so we can
get an early start.'

Hamilton Island astounded Sidonie with its high-rise
buildings, shops, hotels, airport, harbour and the like.

'After all those uninhabited islands, I can't believe
it,' she said as *Morning Mist* was tied up to a berth
in the marina.

'It comes as a bit of a surprise,' Mike agreed, 'but
from a yachtie's point of view, at least, it's a cyclone-

proof harbour, a handy place to re-provision and it's always buzzing with life and fun. Tell you what,' he said, taking in her dazed expression and wide eyes, 'we might postpone your departure until tomorrow.'

'But I——'

'No, Sid—look, I'm going ashore for a short while. Just stay put.' And with that he departed.

Sidonie occupied herself with her packing while he was away, and the tremulous state of her state of mind. Was there any point in delaying the inevitable? she asked herself, and decided there wasn't. So I'll just stick to my guns and go today...

But he was back before she'd finished packing and he threw an airline ticket down on the island counter.

'What's this?' she asked.

'I've booked you a flight tomorrow from here to Melbourne via Brisbane.'

'But I might not be able to afford that,' she protested. 'I was actually planning to go by coach from Proserpine or somewhere like that on the mainland; I'm sure it would be much cheaper!'

'It might be but Proserpine to Melbourne is not far short of two thousand miles; you'd be exhausted. And I'm paying for this.'

'No.' Sidonie stared up into his eyes. 'No, Mike,' she said. 'I couldn't accept it. For one thing, well, I don't know how *you're* placed financially, but, even so, I know you've made the gesture because you feel sorry for me and I *hate* that.'

'All the same, if I have to put you on that plane myself, I will, friend Sid,' he warned with an odd little glint in his blue eyes that made her lips part and her eyes widen.

'You couldn't—you wouldn't do that. Would you?' she said uncertainly.

'Yes, I would. And for today I've hired a buggy and we'll do the sights of Hamilton Island. Don't argue, Sid, just bring your hat and sunscreen—oh, one other thing.' He looked at her with a faint frown in his eyes. 'Where did you plan to stay when you arrive down there?'

'I...I...' She stopped and started again with an effort to quell the turmoil of her emotions. 'I don't quite know. I haven't, well, had a chance to think about it——'

'Then start thinking,' he ordered.

She sat down suddenly and put her hands to her face. 'I...'

He sat down opposite her and said more gently, 'Have you got any girlfriends who could put you up for a few nights until you get—established?'

Sidonie brightened. 'Yes, one. We were at school together and she's got a flat so I don't suppose she'd mind. Why didn't I think of that?'

'You're not renowned for your practicality, that's all. Give her a ring now. Have you got her number?'

'I know it off by heart but I couldn't use the seaphone; it probably costs the earth——'

'Don't worry about that——'

'No, Mike,' Sidonie said with real distress in her eyes. 'She'll be at work anyway. I'll ring her tonight from a phone booth. I'm sure there must be some ashore.'

He stared at her then relented. 'All right.' He touched her chin briefly. 'Don't look so tragic, though, Miss Livingstone. This may not be your favourite kind of exploring, what we're about to do, but I guarantee it might surprise you.'

Hamilton provided quite a few surprises. A fauna park for one thing, a golf driving range on the opposite side of the island, performing dolphins in a pool, a variety of shops and restaurants from a bakery and fishmongers to the boutique Tim Molloy's Karen had mentioned, which was quite mind-boggling in range and price-wise and even sold fur coats.

They came across this and other shops in the resort complex after a late lunch which he'd treated her to in the beach bar and grill, saying they deserved some sustenance after all the sightseeing they'd done. It overlooked Catseye Beach, and the only sad moment she had allowed herself was when she saw some sails in the distance.

But she'd perked up by the time they were wandering down the shopping arcade, and she stopped dead in front of the boutique.

'What?' Mike queried.

'That hat.'

'That one? It's a beauty,' he agreed gravely.

Sidonie stared at the lovely big straw hat with its upturned brim and garland of lush, full flowers. 'I've got the awful feeling I have to have it,' she said hollowly. 'It doesn't happen to me often—I don't think it's ever happened to me before over clothes—well, except those bikinis but that wasn't quite the same thing—but I just know I'll be miserable without that hat. Would you have any idea how much hats like that cost?' she added nervously.

'Let's go and ask.'

'I...no, I don't think we should because you might be tempted to buy it for me, and that I could not bear,' she said with utter determination.

'Sidonie, we'll go in and ask.'

'Fifty dollars,' the sleek, attractive but friendly assistant said.

Sidonie swallowed.

'Why don't you try it on?' the girl coaxed. 'I've got the feeling it's just your hat. There.' She put it on Sidonie's head quite straight, fluffed her hair out a bit beneath it and said with genuine admiration, 'It suits you to a T! And I tell you what, I'll let it go for forty—we've got a new consignment coming in shortly and I'll be pushed for space.'

Sidonie stared at herself and blinked because she fully expected this new image of herself to disappear in the blink of an eyelid, this up-market, updated image that was as modern and attractive as many of the girls she'd seen today. 'I'll take it,' she said huskily and, without bothering to remove the hat, dug hastily into her purse and pressed two twenty-dollar notes on the girl before Mike could do anything.

He was still looking amused as they left the shop— she was still wearing the hat. 'If I've ever seen a case of love at first sight, this is it,' he murmured. 'I trust you won't attempt to sleep in it?'

'Not on your life! I'm going to cherish this hat,' she said jauntily, and stopped to admire her reflection in a plate-glass window. 'By the way,' she added, turning to him, 'thank you for a lovely day.'

He smiled. 'You're easily pleased, kid.'

But the day wasn't over because they discovered Tim Molloy and Karen sitting nonchalantly in the cockpit of *Morning Mist* drinking beer.

Mike groaned. 'I thought we'd given you two the slip.'

'Is that any way to greet an old friend?' Tim complained. 'You didn't tell us you were coming into Hamilton by the way!'

'We weren't but—Sidonie is going home tomorrow.'

'And we've just farewelled our friends so we're at a bit of a loose end—I say, why don't we have dinner at Mariner's tonight? What do you reckon, Sid? On your last night. And I must tell you that's a simply smashing hat!'

It was a mixed experience for Sidonie, her last night. Perhaps easier than spending it alone with Mike, she thought, but of course in her heart of hearts she would have loved to do just that. Then there was the surprise of Mike in a pair of well-cut jeans, and a navy blue, long-sleeved shirt and beautiful, hand-made, by the look of them, polished brown leather shoes—and with his hair trimmed.

'I don't recognise you!' she'd said when he'd come back from the barber's shop.

He'd grimaced. 'It was certainly overdue.'

It was certainly something else too, she decided when they were both ready. The combination of good clothes and short hair took his already compelling looks into the realm of a highly sophisticated man of the world, something she was later to notice was not lost on Karen.

She herself wore her special dress, as she thought of it, and left her hair loose. The dress was in a polished cotton Liberty print, tiny red and white flowers on a dark green background with a heart-shaped neckline, puffed sleeves and a full skirt. It might not

have been the height of fashion but she loved the swirl
of the skirt about her legs, she wore red leather flatties
with it—and she didn't realise that she looked no more
than eighteen in it.

Indeed the ghost of a smile touched his lips as his
eyes rested on her.

She raised an eyebrow. 'No good?'

'On the contrary, it becomes you perfectly.'

She relaxed and smiled widely. 'It's my favourite
dress. I've actually had it for years but I only wear it
on special occasions.'

'It would go well with your hat too—shall we sur-
render ourselves to the Molloy party?'

'Why not?'

The Molloy party was in good form considering
there were only two of them. Karen was especially
animated and looked stunning in a scarlet trouser suit
that set off her dark looks spectacularly, and Tim was
his usual outsize, genial self.

But Sidonie couldn't help wondering if he was unaware that Karen had been somewhat bowled over by
Mike in a new way, although she'd recovered her poise
immediately.

Yet it was a friendly, lively meal and, of course,
because of the proximity of yacht-race week, Hamilton
was buzzing, causing Sidonie some more amazement.
There were people everywhere, there was a band
playing in the bandstand and people dancing in the
street—one wild and woolly-looking young man even
approached her and asked her to dance with him and
she was quite relieved when Mike took her hand in
his from then on as they strolled back to the boat.

It was Tim's and Karen's farewells that undid her
a bit then. Mike had invited them on board for coffee

but when they stood up to leave Tim gave her a bear-hug, told her that if ever she needed some orthodontistry to be sure and go and see him, he'd give her a cut rate—they'd discovered that Melbourne was their mutual home town—and Karen had hugged her warmly as well, and for some strange reason it brought tears to her eyes.

Of course she hid them on the pretext of blowing her nose but once they'd gone Mike said, 'You made quite a hit with those two despite your awful suspicions about them.'

'I know, that was silly of me, I guess,' she said huskily, shadows of tiredness and strain touching her face.

And she thought she discerned an odd expression in his eyes before he seemed to relax deliberately, and say, 'Bed for you, I think, my dear. You've got a big day tomorrow.'

She nodded. 'Goodnight—I'm not going to bother you with any emotional farewells tomorrow.' She tried to smile. 'So I'll just say thanks now, for *everything*.' And she turned away immediately. He didn't stop her or say anything further.

It occurred to her as she lay in her bunk for the last time that she couldn't be entirely sad, although she certainly was hauntingly so for the most part. But there was also a part of her that could never regret loving Mike Brennan, it seemed. She tried to work it out as she lay in a still, small mound beneath the covers—and decided it almost came naturally to her, just like breathing. And as such it appeared to involve a deep concern for his welfare which so obviously didn't lie with her. But it translates to this, she reflected; I couldn't help but be happy to know he was happy, I can't change the way I feel and it seems to be a good thing that's happened to me; maybe that sounds crazy but I can't help it. So if I hold on to that...perhaps I'll be able to get through...whatever comes next.

It was a hot, bright morning as they sat side by side in the small airport terminal and watched happy holiday-makers stream off the jet that would shortly be winging her away south.

It was also obvious to her that Mike was not in a good mood and she had the feeling it had to do with what she wore—the same outfit she'd had on the day they'd met.

'Mike,' she said patiently but flickered him a wary little glance, 'I know you told me not to wear these kind of clothes, and if it makes you happier I'll throw them away when I get home, but it's the only sensible outfit I've got for flying to Melbourne—it could be freezing down there. So you see, I can be practical if I have to.'

He turned to look at her in silence for a long moment—at the high-buttoned collar of her thick white cotton shirt, then her face, which had acquired the faintest golden bloom from the sun, her hair not in a bun but tied back tidily, the hound's-tooth skirt and flat black shoes and her bag and boarding-card clutched in her hands, her new hat set carefully on the vacant chair beside her. Then he smiled perfunctorily. 'I know.'

'Good. I wouldn't like to think you were cross with me.'

He said something inaudible and the flight was called. Sidonie stood up. She'd rehearsed this moment

her mind ever since waking up and she steeled
herself to do it exactly as she'd rehearsed. She held
out her hand to him and said with a wry little smile,
'Take care of *Morning Mist*, Mike, and yourself. Bye!'

He stood up, paused, then took her hand in his.
'Goodbye, sweet Sid. You take care too.' He released
her hand.

'I will!' She picked up her hat, turned away and,
as an afterthought—she hadn't rehearsed this—looked
down at it in her hands then put it on her head
thinking that it might look quite inappropriate, even
silly with what she wore, but she didn't care. It was
her one souvenir not only of the trip but of Mike,
and somehow it strengthened her spirit to wear it.

She walked away without a backward glance with
her shoulders square and her beautiful hat square on
her head. She'd barely shown them her boarding-pass
and was about to step out into the sunlight when she
felt a pair of hands on her shoulders, and Mike
Brennan swung her round and said in a furiously
loaded voice, 'What the *hell* am I going to do with
you, Sidonie Hill?'

Her mouth dropped open and the flowers on her
hat bobbed. 'I don't know what you mean...'

His blue eyes blazed. 'I mean that I just can't let
you go, damn it!'

CHAPTER FIVE

'MIKE!' she whispered, going red then pale. 'I——'

'And do you know why?' he said savagely, his fingers digging into her thin shoulders. 'My conscience wouldn't give me a minute's bloody peace. I'd be worried about you finding a job, finding somewhere to stay—falling into a pond and drowning yourself, for that matter, or simply starving.'

The little pulse of hope that had fluttered in Sidonie's heart died. 'I——'

'So for what it's worth you can help me take the boat back to Tin Can Bay and somehow or other along the way we'll hammer out a plan for the rest of your life and generally improve your basic survival skills so that I won't ever have to watch you walk away again and feel as guilty as hell!'

She found her tongue. 'You don't have to feel guilty about me. How do you think I feel now? Like some sort of Orphan Annie, like some kind of *stray* you've taken pity on, and it's horrible!'

'Well, you'd better just get used to it,' he replied brutally.

'Er——' a voice said behind them and Sidonie looked around wildly, to discover there was a whole group of exceedingly interested people about them because they were blocking the exit.

'Mike...' She had some difficulty with her voice but the underlying plea was unmistakable. 'Don't do this to me. Anyway my bag's already on the plane and——'

'We'll get it off.' He released her shoulders but took her hand in a vice-like grip and turned to the uniformed official behind them. 'Sorry, mate,' he said with not the least trace of apology in his voice, 'but we've had a change of plan. Could you help us to retrieve this person's luggage?'

'This person' sat in a furious, trembling silence as she was driven back by buggy to the marina, had her hand once again taken in a strong grip and was given no option but to board *Morning Mist*.

'And what's more,' Mike Brennan said to her when they were in the main cabin, his eyes still smouldering, 'you won't ever wear that outfit again because I'll personally throw it away as soon as you've changed.'

'I *hate* you——'

'We both know you don't,' he overrode her but in more dispassionate tones, 'so you might as well get changed, friend Sid. And then we'll start making plans for Tin Can Bay.'

She sat, about half an hour later, in a stern silence on the back of the boat. She'd changed into her white shorts and a blue and white spotted blouse and braided her hair into a plait. She had her arms around her knees and she was staring into space, not only feeling stern—numb and frozen was a better description— but also disbelieving.

'Here,' Mike said, and put a cup of tea accompanied by a fresh chocolate éclair down beside her. 'We need to talk.'

'The mind boggles,' she said tautly.

'You said that to me once before,' he commented equably. 'It didn't stop you coming with me then.'

Sidonie muttered something incomprehensible and, because she was afraid she might start to cry, she took a sip of tea then a large bite of éclair.

'I'm sorry if I offended you this morning, Sid,' he said gravely. 'You have some cream on your chin.'

She wiped her chin with considerable chagrin. 'Offended me?' she marvelled. 'If you must know I can't ever recall feeling more of a fool.'

'Still, I think it would help us both if we cleared the air,' he murmured. 'So you go first.'

'I told you how I felt at the airport. Nothing, so far, has made me change my mind,' she said bitterly.

'Is that,' he said in a deceptively idle way, 'because for a moment there you were tempted to hope I was proposing a—closer relationship between us?'

It was too much. She swung round with angry tears she couldn't hide glittering in her eyes and said fiercely, 'Don't—just don't mention that to me ever again, Mike Brennan. It has to be about as low as anyone can go.'

'Look, Sid,' he said evenly, 'I did what I did in the heat of the moment.' He paused and stared at her, taking in her pallor and the way her mouth worked as she valiantly tried to stem the tears. 'For some strange reason it was the way you put on that hat that did it. It was ... about the most gallant gesture I've ever seen and it negated every damned bit of good sense I've been offering myself for—days. So—no,' he said drily, as she made to interrupt, 'let me finish, let me lay my cards on the table. I *can't* offer you love and there are a whole lot of reasons for that, but I can offer you friendship for a while and perhaps I can even help you to sort your life out a bit.'

Her lips parted. 'How?' she whispered.

'I have some contacts in Melbourne, in the aircraft maintenance industry as a matter of fact. In light of how fascinating you find diesel motors I'm sure jet engines would delight you.'

Her eyes were suddenly huge then she blinked confusedly and swallowed several times.

'Drink your tea and finish your éclair,' he said wryly.

She did as she was bid then said through a mouthful of éclair, 'I—I beg your pardon——' she swallowed again hastily '—I don't know what to say.'

His lips twisted. 'Yes would do it. Although,' he sobered, 'you said something to me the other day about not being a lost cause. Believe me, Sid, I am, in that way.' And his eyes were a deep, penetrating blue.

'Could you tell me why?' The words were out before she could stop them so she decided fatalistically that she might as well go on. 'I mean, is it only me or—well, is it only me? I——' she shook her head and gestured vigorously '—I promise I won't be offended.'

'No,' he said rather gently, 'it's not *only* you although that has something to do with it. I might as well be light-years away from you in experience as well as a good few years ahead in age. I...' He stopped and looked into the distance.

'Would it be fair to say you prefer your women older and more sophisticated?' she suggested after a time.

He brought his gaze back to her then smiled reluctantly and with some irony. 'Something like that but——'

She forestalled him. 'I understand completely. Please don't worry about me being totally *demolished*, incidentally. I'm ...' she paused and wondered how to put it '... I'm very resilient for one thing and——' she looked down at her hands '—despite all my other failings not an *insensitive* sort of person.' She looked up and smiled at him. 'I feel better already. So if you're really sure you want to take me along, should we look at the charts?'

He stared at her, seemed about to say something then changed his mind and said, 'You'd better ring your friend in Melbourne; use the sea-phone, it actually doesn't cost a lost. It's also Saturday—will she be home?'

'Yes ...'

But their departure was delayed by a week firstly by a strong-wind warning then the discovery that the auto-pilot was amiss and they had to get an electronics expert from the mainland who disconnected it and took it away with him for repairs.

It was obvious that this turn of events was causing Mike to chafe at the bit, and equally obvious that Tim Molloy, not to mention Karen, who were staying at the Hamilton Towers hotel for race week, now upon them, were delighted—at first, that was. Because it then became obvious that Karen had set her sights on Mike.

Perhaps she can't help herself, Sidonie tried to think charitably, and anyway it's none of my business. But as that hectic week passed with all the excitement of the racing and associated parties, Tim started to get deflated, Mike more than ever inscrutable and Karen—well, she glowed and became even more sultry and attractive.

It was probably inevitable that things should come to a head one night and that it should be a dance party that would do it. Sidonie hadn't wanted to go but Tim had insisted they all go and Mike shrugged non-committally. She wore her special dress but Karen looked spectacular in emerald-green diaphanous harem pants, a tiny top, long gold earrings, gold shoes and gold belt.

Why are you doing this, Tim? Sidonie asked him silently on the veranda above Mariner's as the music pulsed and dancers began to take to the floor. But Tim got up with every appearance of a jovial man with not a thing on his mind and took Karen away to dance. Mike stared over the veranda at the cluster of masts in the moonlight then said to her with a brief smile, but a totally moody expression in his eyes. 'Do you dance, Sid?'

She swallowed a bit uncertainly. 'I do and I don't.'

'I might have known it would be complicated,' he murmured with a lift of an eyebrow. 'Would you care to explain?'

She pursed her lips. 'I can do the sailors' hornpipe and the Highland fling. I'm not much good at anything else.'

He blinked. 'Where, one hesitates to enquire, did you learn those two?'

'A sailor taught me the hornpipe and a Scot the Highland fling. Which seems to me the obvious way to go about it,' she added innocently.

He laughed and she relaxed. 'They were both friends of my father and I was about six at the time. I—er—that was another thing that got me into trouble during my brief stint as a teacher.'

'You taught them to dance as well as play poker?'

'Yes. It wasn't greatly appreciated.' She grimaced.

'What did they come up with this time? That you could be turning them into compulsive dancers?'

She grinned. 'No, they said it was highly disruptive—it is actually very difficult to do either of those dances without making a lot of noise.'

'I believe you.' He stopped and looked up as Karen and Tim returned.

'A round of drinks, everyone? It's my shout,' Tim said immediately and lumbered off to the bar.

But Karen slid her hand across the table and said huskily, 'Dance with me, Mike?'

He looked into her dark eyes with his own narrowed for a long moment then got up without a word.

Sidonie sat back and watched them, her thoughts in a tangle, and more so when Tim came back, sized up the situation and sat down despondently. And it was impossible not to go on watching Mike and Karen because it soon became obvious they were the best dancers as well as the most spectacular couple on the floor. And there was something in the way Mike looked down at Karen and in the way his hands lingered on her body that told its own tale.

Sidonie did look away at last and opened her mouth to say something comforting to Tim, but she closed it because what could you say? And anyway, at that same moment, some people he knew walked past and he hailed them and insisted they sit down and have a drink. So she got introduced as his little friend Sid but not long afterwards was able to slip away quietly.

She took a few deep breaths on the pavement and then on an impulse hailed a cruising shuttle, discovered it was going to the other side of the island and went for a ride.

It was quiet as she wandered through the main resort complex with nearly all of the action taking place on the harbourside tonight, she guessed, and she walked out to the dolphin pool and stood on the bridge looking out to sea. And she tried to tell herself she shouldn't worry, she shouldn't care but it didn't help although eventually the peace and cool night air lessened her feeling of distress and she decided to walk back up over the hill to the boat.

The music was still booming and pulsing as she walked past Mariner's but it was as she came to the grassy slope overlooking the harbour known as Hesperus Park that she noticed Tim sitting on the lawn with his head in his hands. She hesitated then sighed, and went to sit down beside him.

'Tim,' she said tentatively, 'are you all right?'

He looked up blearily. 'Well, if it isn't my little friend Sid! We make a good pair, don't we? Both stood up in a manner of speaking.'

'Not really—well, not me.' Sidonie bit her lip. 'I mean to say, I had no expectations . . .' She tailed off awkwardly.

'I'd like to make a bet you're as smitten with him as all the others, though.'

Sidonie thought of lying but it didn't seem fair. 'I do love him,' she said seriously. 'But it's a bit different—I know he could never be for me, you see. So I mostly worry about him being happy—it's very hard to explain.'

'I wouldn't say Karen feels the same,' Tim said bitterly then sighed heavily. 'I bought her that outfit, you know. Not that she needed me to buy her clothes but as soon as I saw it I could see her in it, and now... Bitch,' he said helplessly.

'I must admit I wondered—no.' Sidonie changed tack and tried again. 'He'll probably sail away and that will be that. He...I don't know a lot about him,' she confessed, 'but he strikes me as real loner.'

Tim rubbed his face then said, 'He is a real loner. That's why he has to fight girls off; they just can't bear it,' he said cynically. 'And when they know what he does for a living it gets worse.'

'What does he do for a living?' Sidonie asked cautiously.

Tim laughed a little unkindly. 'I got the message he hadn't told you. Did you really think he bums around the South Pacific nursing other people's boats for them, little Sid? He's the ace test pilot for a huge overseas aircraft manufacturer. He's the best, most naturally gifted God-damned pilot I've ever seen. He's got no nerves, he thrives on the unexpected—and that's a natural turn-on for most women, dangerous men doing dangerous jobs—until they try to pin him down to walking up the aisle with them, that is. But is it any wonder being even a glorified dentist falls down by comparison?'

'Oh!' Sidonie whispered, her eyes huge. 'So...' Words failed her briefly. 'I mean, what's he doing now?'

'He takes a couple of months off every year and gets into yachting as a form of relaxation. And gradually, over the years, he's upgraded his boats to this one. Not short of a quid either, is our Mike. But he doesn't like too many people, particularly of the female persuasion, to know that either.'

'I see.' Sidonie expelled a deep breath and felt her face redden for several reasons. 'Do I look like a fortune huntress to you, Tim?' she said indignantly finally.

'Not you, Sid,' Tim said wryly and gave her a little hug. Then he sighed again to the depths of his being. 'But you can never tell with most women,' he added bleakly.

'That's not a nice thing to say, Tim,' she said quietly.

'I'm not feeling very nice,' he commented. 'And look at Karen—she was quite happy for me to spend money on her for all that I didn't have to...' He swore beneath his breath.

'It seems to me Mike is a little bit to blame too,' she said with a frown.

'Because I'm a friend of his? You're right but unfortunately—oh, well, I might as well tell you the whole caboodle! You see, Mike fell in love with a girl once, seriously in love with her, and she with him. But she couldn't bear what he did; she wanted him to settle down to a nine-to-five job and come home to her and the kids, once they came, every evening. She didn't realise you can't change a bloke like Mike, you can't clip his wings, so it all ground to a halt because she got this stupid idea in her head that if he really loved her he'd be happy to do it.' He shook his head.

'She doesn't sound like a very wise person,' Sidonie ventured.

'Who is when it comes to love? I tried to tell her but she wouldn't listen. And one day she went out and married someone else, something I think she's regretted ever since.'

'How...do you know all this, Tim?'

'Because she happens to be my sister,' he said morosely.

Sidonie stared at him. 'Oh, Tim, it wasn't your fault, though.'

'No, although I was the idiot who introduced them to each other in the first place. But I just can't help feeling a bit responsible, which is why, I suppose, if it had been anyone else but bloody Mike Brennan, I'd be wanting to punch his face in.' He breathed agitatedly.

'I don't think that's a good idea at all,' Sidonie said hurriedly. 'Tim,' she added gently, 'perhaps Karen is just not the one for you.'

'Sid——' he turned to her '—when the hell does that ever make any difference?'

Which, of course, was something she had no answer for. So after a time she suggested that they couldn't sit in the park all night and asked him what he wanted to do.

'Go back to the boat, I guess,' he said and lurched a bit unsteadily to his feet. 'She can have the hotel room for whatever she's got in mind! She can also find her own way off this bloody island—don't be surprised if *you* find yourself flying back after all tomorrow, Sid!'

She said nothing and they walked to the marina together and she made sure he got aboard his boat without falling into Hamilton Harbour and wrung a promise from him that he would take himself to bed. It was all she could do and she was somewhat re-assured that he wasn't in any condition to do much else himself.

But it was a long time before she fell asleep as she grappled with all she'd found out—and Mike didn't return to the boat.

She woke at the crack of dawn, though, as *Morning Mist* rocked gently, and she knew it was Mike. So she lay for a time, wondering what to do, and when she heard no further sounds she thought he might have taken himself to bed and she got up, dressed, and went out to make herself a cup of tea.

But he was sitting at the island counter, staring into space.

'Oh! Sorry, I thought you...' She stopped awkwardly.

He turned his head briefly, his eyes faintly amused. 'Good morning, Sid. You thought I'd what?'

'Er—gone to bed.' She twisted her hands.

He looked at her again, for longer this time, taking in her yellow shirt and blue shorts, her neat hair and scrubbed face. 'I probably should,' he said at last and fingered the faint blue shadows on his jaw. 'And take my sins with me,' he added with soft mockery.

'That's got nothing to do with me, Mike,' she said although her eyes were distressed, 'but if you'd like me to...move out I will.'

He'd started to stretch but stopped halfway. 'Why the hell would I want you to do that?'

'I just thought—I—well, I wondered if there mightn't be some new—arrangements now,' she finished somewhat exasperatedly and looked at him, annoyed.

'You mean you thought I'd want to replace you with Karen?'

'*Yes.*'

'Of which you don't approve at all, I take it?'

'It's not my place to approve or disapprove,' she said stiffly, 'but I think it's a lousy thing to do to a friend.'

'If I've done anything to Tim, I've done him a favour, friend Sid,' he said with considerable irony. 'But I have no intention of replacing you with anyone at this stage. Moreover, they called me up yesterday to tell me the auto-pilot is going again and they'll be putting it back in this morning, so we'll be leaving directly it's done. I anticipate that to be around ten hundred hours, Miss Hill.'

Sidonie stared at him with her lips parted. 'Do you mean to tell me,' she said finally, 'that you've broken up Tim and Karen, spent the night with her by all appearances and that's all there is to it?'

'Sid,' he said with a gentle kind of humour that was curiously lethal, 'more or less but only time will tell whether I've broken them up.'

'But...' She couldn't go on.

'You feel Karen deserves better despite the fact that she was quite happy to come straight from his arms to mine?' he queried.

'No...I mean...you shouldn't have let her! You're as bad as she is!'

'Quite possibly,' he agreed wryly.

'I think this is terrible,' Sidonie whispered.

'I wonder why I knew you would?' he said drily. 'But perhaps it could be a salutary lesson for you, Sid. Maybe now you'll really understand why you and I wouldn't deal too well together at all.'

'Because you...because you...' The words stuck in her throat.

'Because I'm a disillusioned cynic? Yes.' He picked up a set of keys from the counter and fiddled with them in his long fingers for a time. 'Because it suited me to take advantage of what was being so blatantly offered but strictly on my terms—is that what you're trying to say?'

She could only stare at him with tears pricking her eyelids.

He threw the keys away from him and stood up. 'For God's sake don't cry,' he said roughly. 'Anyone would think you were the keeper of my soul.'

'No.' She sniffed. 'But I wouldn't be surprised if you didn't quite like yourself at the moment, Mike Brennan,' she added with a level look despite the brightness of her eyes. 'But I'll say no more. Would you like a cup of tea?'

'Thanks—and thank you for that small mercy—no more sermons, I mean.'

She tossed her head and compressed her lips as she went behind the counter and started the tea. It took about five minutes and there was dead silence as he resumed his seat, looking moodier than she'd ever seen him, also drained and disenchanted and as if he'd like nothing more than to be shot of the whole situation.

But still she said nothing as she slid a cup and saucer towards him. It was he who broke the silence.

'I may not quite like myself at the moment,' he said abruptly, 'but what *you* might not understand, Sid, is that those are the games someone like me plays with women, willing women. If you imagine Karen will be at all demolished, perish the thought, my dear,' he said curtly. 'If she doesn't worm her way back into Tim's embrace, she'll find someone else. Whereas you haven't got the faintest idea what it's about and would only get terribly hurt. I'm going to bed.' And he ignored his tea and walked away, with deadly impatience stamped into every line of his body, to his cabin.

'All right, take her out. I'll set the foresail.'

It was eleven hundred hours actually as *Morning Mist* slid out of Hamilton Harbour with Sid at the wheel. Mike had slept for a couple of hours then disappeared—to make his peace with Tim Molloy, Sid had hoped, but had no way of knowing. He'd come back laden down with fresh fruit and vegetables, fresh bread and some of the bakery's famous meat pies, and the auto-pilot man had arrived at the same time so that their opportunity for conversation had been severely limited. Which was just as well, she thought. I wouldn't know what to say to him or even if there's anything I want to say to him at all. But she'd been unable to help wondering whether Karen would appear on the scene and what kind of a fuss might ensue— she was by no means as certain as Mike that Karen would be willing to play this particular game by his rules. But there'd been no sign of her and she'd breathed a sigh of relief.

So what happens now? she wondered as she cleared the wall and entrance leads and steered the yacht into the Dent Passage—and discovered herself feeling a little shell-shocked.

'Sid!'

'Yes?'

'You'll have us aground if you're not careful— haven't you got the chart with you?' he called from amidships where he was making preparations to hoist the mainsail.

'No. Oh! Sorry, I must have been dreaming...' She swung the wheel.

'*Sid*,' he yelled, then muttered to himself, left the sail and came back to the cockpit. 'What's the matter?' He took the wheel out of her hands. 'Can't you see that sign? It's there for the express purpose of preventing yachts from catching aircraft on their masts. That's the end of the runway, you little idiot!'

'I'm sorry,' she said confusedly. 'Of course it is. I just feel a bit—I don't know.' She swallowed. 'I think it's all been a bit much for me...'

He cast her a narrowed, intent look. 'Do you want to go back? Is that what you're trying to say?'

'No... No, but...'

'Are you quite sure, Sidonie?' he said through his teeth.

She took a deep breath and closed her eyes. After a moment she opened them and said steadily, 'Yes. I'm fine now. You can put the sail up, I'll turn her into the wind.'

Half an hour later they'd cleared the passage, set a course and he came down into the cabin and looked at her rather intently as she sat at the chart table. 'How do you feel now?'

'F... quite good. Sorry about that. I see you've changed your mind about Scawfell.'

'Yes—I've been thinking, the long-range forecast is good, the winds are right—north-easterlies—there'll be some moon—I'm tempted to run through the night and however long it takes.'

Her eyes widened. 'Where to?'

'Middle Percy.' He glanced at her with that same narrowed look, however.

But Sidonie's eyes suddenly shone with excitement. 'What an adventure,' she said in a hushed voice. 'Does that mean we'll have to take turns at the watch and so on? Do you plan to sail all the way?'

'If possible, and dodge all the islands and reefs in between,' he teased. 'But I've done it before. Of course how far we can sail without motoring at all depends on the wind and whether we need to get out of any heavy conditions that can crop up despite the most favourable forecasts. Still on, Sid?'

'I couldn't think of anything I'd like to do more,' she said with a sudden wide, eager smile.

He grimaced and patted her on the head. 'You're a strange kid, Sid. Am I forgiven?'

She sobered.

'Perhaps I shouldn't have asked,' he said ruefully.

'Mike,' she tried to choose her words with care but then shrugged a little defeatedly, 'perhaps you're right. There could be lots of things I don't understand.'

'And some things I hope you never do,' he said drily. 'Well, shall we devise a roster? And I'll take you through the charts; we can put our way-points into the GPS and generally prepare ourselves for this voyage of—discovery.'

CHAPTER SIX

THE next couple of days were the most exciting of Sidonie's life. There were nights of moonlight on a dark sea, of being totally in charge while Mike slept; the shush of *Morning Mist* slicing through the swell of a pink-tinged dawn, of islands that came and went, birds that crossed their path, spray on her face, salt on her skin and exultation in her heart.

Days of working with parallel rulers and dividers as well as precision instruments such as the GPS, compass and radar, which were all she had to guide her at night although Mike had started to teach her about the stars and celestial navigation.

Days of watching a master at work as Mike set the sails to gain the maximum benefit from a wind that sometimes dropped to below ten knots, sometimes swung round to the south and slowed them right down to barely moving. A master who seemed to know by heart about the cross-currents and tidal sets in the area and could usually identify any blip on the radar at a glance. Days and hours of watching him slough off the moodiness and that alter ego of a devastatingly attractive, sophisticated but hard and withdrawn man who had turned Karen's head so completely, who had used her perhaps no more than she deserved, but all the same . . .

Lovely days.

'I'm getting so good at this I can't believe it!' Sidonie said excitedly as she placed a perfectly cooked meal of scrambled eggs and bacon before him on their second morning. 'I know it's pretty basic but all the same.'

'All the same indeed,' he murmured, his eyes laughing at her. He'd just done a four-hour watch from three to seven, the darkness to dawn one, as they called it, and his jaw was blue with stubble, his eyes tired despite their amusement. 'You're looking pretty bright for someone who did the graveyard watch, Sid.'

She grimaced. 'I read poetry to keep me awake.'

'I've always found one has to be particularly awake in the first place to do that.'

'This was Edward Lear and I read it out aloud. Nonsense *should* be read out aloud, I feel. Did you know he was the youngest of twenty-one children?'

Mike raised an eyebrow. 'No—that could certainly bring out a nonsensical streak in one.'

'Well, I've wondered about that.' Sidonie paused and waved a forkful of bacon thoughtfully. 'As an only child myself, I've often thought I might have been a more practical person if I'd had some brothers and sisters, but if you go on Lear it doesn't seem to work that way. But then again he could have been both practical and had this marvellous streak of nonsense; I don't know.'

He pushed his plate away and reached for the coffee-pot. 'I wouldn't worry about it too much. In some respects, mechanically-wise, for example, you're extremely level-headed. And you can be trusted to do a graveyard watch on your own, and even come up smiling and with breakfast after only four hours of kip. That,' he said seriously, 'is a very worthy attribute in a girl.'

'And that,' she said with a mischievous little smile, 'is a bit like being damned with faint praise for any self-respecting girl, although of course I appreciate it entirely.'

He laughed. 'Sorry. I——'

But she wouldn't let him go on. 'I was only teasing,' she said gently.

His eyes softened as they rested on her. 'By the way,' he said after a moment, 'I was serious about trying to get you a job—you're probably wondering what contacts I have; I won't bore you with them but they're there.'

'Mike——' Sidonie took a deep breath '—I have to tell you Tim told me what you do for a living. I wasn't going to mention it but now it seems sneaky to pretend I don't know although I gather you'd much rather I *didn't* know.' She frowned. 'That sounds awfully convoluted, doesn't it? But do you know what I mean?'

'When did he tell you this?'

'When he was feeling rather maudlin and had had too much to drink. I——'

'I suppose he told you about his sister as well,' he said drily. 'He can always be relied upon to trot that out when he gets drunk.'

'Yes, well, he did. But that's got nothing to do with me. If you *could* help me to get a job, though, I'd really appreciate it—and I won't say another word on the subject,' she concluded hastily.

'Do you mean to tell me it doesn't arouse the slightest curiosity in you, what I do for a living, Sid?' he drawled.

'Well, that would be a lie—were I to tell you that,' she said cautiously. 'But it wouldn't be a lie to say that it hasn't aroused what Tim described as the fatal fascination that causes women to throw themselves at your feet, or words to that effect, in me. For two reasons: something like that had already happened to me, as we both know, although we've dealt with it and resolved it, and secondly, it's probably very much like any other job, at times boring and repetitive. And possibly not as dangerous nowadays as a lot of people think,' she said prosaically.

He stared at her then a reluctant smile twisted his lips. 'Talk about being damned with faint praise,' he murmured, 'but of course you're right, Sid.'

'Then——' she looked at him gravely '—is it all right to talk about it? I won't if you don't want to or if it's going to make you moody and—whatever, only the thing is, I'd very much like to know a bit about it. What it's like finding an aircraft's limiting Mach number for example, whether you prefer to fly subsonic or supersonic planes, how much of the draughting and designing you're involved in before you actually test the prototype. And, while I may have sounded a bit withering about the danger, I'm sure there can be *some*, and some absolutely thrilling moments too.'

'Out of the mouths of babes,' he said and shook his head wryly. Then added, 'Am I very often moody and—whatever? Downright bloody-minded perhaps?'

She considered. 'I wouldn't say that.'

'Thank you,' he replied with irony. But he went on, 'There are two kinds of flying—the really high-tech stuff, and the simple pleasure of taking up a single-engine light plane. I enjoy both and, if you really want to know about Mach percentages, pass me a pencil and a piece of paper. It's all to do with the speed of sound or the sound barrier and how close a subsonic aircraft that hasn't been designed to fly through it can get to it before it becomes uncontrollable.'

An hour later he pushed the bit of paper away and stretched but Sidonie was glowing. 'It's absolutely fascinating, isn't it?'

'I've always found it so,' he agreed with a straight face.

'Please tell me how you got started,' she begged.

'I joined the air force.'

'Had you always wanted to fly?'

He grimaced. 'Always. Much to my parents' disapproval.'

'Why?' She looked at him wide-eyed.

'My father was an accountant and my mother— well, if she had one abiding passion it was gardens and gardening. They were very settled sort of people; apart from going to work, quite often the most exciting thing they did was their fortnightly visit to the local library. To have produced . . . me always came as a bit of a shock to them, I think.'

'Did they put all sorts of obstacles in your path?' she queried knowledgeably.

'All sorts,' he concurred with a grin.

'So—were you an only child too, Mike?'

'Uh-huh.'

She paused. Then she said with a frown, 'Do you know what I think? I think only children *have* to use their imaginations a lot, which is why we might end up wanting to spread our wings so much and do different things.'

'What about Edward Lear?'

'He could be the exception that proves the rule!'

'He could indeed,' he agreed amusedly.

'So that's why—well, it could also be why you're a bit of a loner,' she said slowly and thoughtfully.

'I bow to your wisdom in these matters, Sid. What makes you think I'm such a loner, though?'

'Aren't you?'

For some reason his eyes narrowed then he shrugged, 'Perhaps.'

She stood up and collected plates. 'And now you should get some sleep. By my calculations we should be abeam of Prudhoe Island shortly and we could even make Middle Percy early this afternoon.'

'You're spot-on, kid.'

But as it happened she wasn't.

She noticed the bank of cloud building to the south-east at about midday, and the eerie way the light north-easterly dropped almost completely—presage often, she knew, to a change, and suspected it might be a vigorous one behind the front of clouds. She also suspected it might have taken the Department of Meteorology by surprise because it hadn't been broadcast on the last weather forecast she'd heard. But even she was unprepared for the swiftness with which it came through, a thirty-knot south-easterly like a bullet, and in a few minutes she had sails flapping and *Morning Mist* slewing untidily in a rising sea.

Fortunately Mike, whom she'd decided to let sleep a bit longer because of the time she'd taken up having the finer points of test piloting explained to her, was up on deck immediately.

'It came really suddenly,' she tried to explain, above the wind.

'Mmm...' He looked around intently. 'Listen, we're in for a rough ride. I'm going to get all these sheets down and try to rig up a storm sail. Start the motor and hold her into the wind as best you can.'

'Romeo,' she said obediently.

'And, while you've got the chance, call up Mackay Air Sea Rescue, give them our position and let them know the conditions—I think our best bet is still to run for Percy; tell them we'll call back if there's any change.'

Thirty tense minutes later he slid into the cockpit beside her and took the wheel. Her fingers were white with strain. 'I've got her.'

'You're soaked.'

'Doesn't matter—well, why don't you pop down into the cabin, make things as fast as you can then bring up a dry shirt and a waterproof?'

'OK.'

'Sid?' he said just as she was about to slip down the ladder. She looked up at him. 'Thanks—for not panicking yet, I mean.'

She blushed with pleasure.

It took them four hours to reach Middle Percy, four highly uncomfortable hours when there were times, she had to be honest, when she was frightened stiff but refused to give way to it. She'd never seen seas as big nor heard a wind howl quite as devilishly; she wasn't sure how, as they slipped into one great trough after another, Mike managed to control *Morning Mist* and guessed it was pure seamanship and strength.

It was all she could do not to burst into tears when the bulk of an island loomed up ahead and he said, 'Middle Percy; we should get some protection under its northern lee but I think, as I hoped, this squall is passing us by now.'

And it wasn't until they were safely anchored under the lee of Middle Percy that she went below, looked around at the chaos, and could restrain the tears no longer.

'Hey,' he said softly, coming down behind her, 'it will clean up, it's only superficial.' He rescued some apples and oranges and began stacking all the books that had fallen out.

She scrubbed at her eyes furiously. 'I'm not really crying.'

'You're allowed to,' he said with a grin. 'Do you think I wasn't scared?'

'You didn't show it.'

'Nevertheless the man who isn't scared of what the sea can do is only an idiot.' He straightened, looked at her anxious expression then came over and hugged her briefly. 'Make us a cup of tea—no, that was definitely a rum and Coke trip in best seafaring traditions. I'll get it. Sit down and relax.'

She didn't, of course. She went on tidying up until he put a glass into her hands and propelled her to the settee. 'We'll stay here a couple of days. I'd like to check the boat out from stem to stern. That was a pretty solid initiation but I thought she handled it well.'

Sidonie brightened. 'I'll help.'

And the rum and Coke helped so that she was able to laugh when she went into her bathroom and discovered her shampoo had not so much leaked but plastered itself liberally over walls, floor and ceiling.

'At least it smells nice,' she said wryly to Mike, 'if a bit overpoweringly so.'

'Mmm... Like a flower garden. Like your hair,' he said lightly. And it was as if her heart moved slightly, like a shy bird ruffling its feathers then going back to sleep.

So they worked all day the next day restoring *Morning Mist* to shipshape, combing the engine, checking the bilges and repairing the self-furling mechanism of the foresail, which had jammed, fortunately after the sail had been furled. But the next day when the wind swung back to a northerly they moved round the island to Whites Bay and had a lay day. They went ashore to explore and Sidonie was fascinated by Middle Percy.

One of the outer islands within the reef and well south of the Whitsundays, it had a different air to it, she told Mike. You really felt you were in the middle of a great ocean; the rocks around the beach and in the bay had strange, wind-eroded shapes and it was one of those exciting places, possibly like visiting Easter Island, she said she felt.

'I don't know about that,' he replied as they climbed a huge smooth sand dune littered with some weird and wonderful silvery driftwood. 'I've never come across any strange stone monoliths with enigmatic expressions.'

'You're being deliberately unromantic,' she teased, and stopped suddenly, her eyes widening as they reached the plateau of the dune. 'Look at that,' she whispered and put her hand into his suddenly. 'That' was a single line of huge footprints in the sand. 'What could it possibly be?'

'Well, now—a yeti?' It was his turn to tease.

'No, Mike, I'm serious,' she said reproachfully. 'Those are not human footprints, they don't come from the beach and there's nothing but scrub then rocks and that peak behind.' She gestured to where the bulk of Middle Percy rose to the skyline.

He laughed. 'I'd love to be able to tell you there's a legend of an Abominable Sandman who lives here but in fact the White family, whom this bay is named after, lived here for years and ran stock on the island—it's probably a very large goat gone bush or a cow.'

She relaxed her grip on his hand a bit and sighed whimsically. 'So much for romance.'

'Well, wild cows and goats can be a bit of a handful, you know.'

'It's not the same,' she said grandly.

But that night, as they sat in the cockpit and the moon shone over the dunes, making them white with black fringes, and curlews cried mournfully, she told him she'd had her faith restored in Middle Percy. 'It's—for some reason, it really gets to me,' she said wonderingly.

'I must admit I have a soft spot for it myself,' he conceded.

They sat in silence and the water lapped gently against the hull and Sidonie thought of the wide dark water around them and was lost in her imaginings, which inexplicably turned sad. Which was probably how, when Mike suggested it was time for bed, she was so preoccupied with an upsurge of grief solely to do with the magic of this world and him as its central pivot that she missed her footing as she went down the ladder, fell, hit her head on the side of the chart table and knocked herself out briefly.

'*Sid*?'

Her lashes fluttered up uncertainly; she discovered she was in his arms in his lap and he was staring down at her with a frown of concern.

'Oh . . .' It all came back to her and she tried to sit up. 'What a stupid thing to do. I don't *think* I've done any damage—I must have been daydreaming,' she said shakenly.

He breathed a sigh of relief. 'Don't,' he said briefly and stilled her urgent movements. 'You could have concussion. Does your head hurt?'

She lay back and felt her head tentatively. There was already a bump above her left temple. 'Not yet—too much,' she said cautiously, and felt his fingers follow the path hers had, find the bump and she winced.

'You're going to have the proverbial lump like an egg for a day or two and a bit of a headache. Any other symptoms like double vision or feeling cold?'

She blinked experimentally. 'No, no double vision.' But she shivered suddenly, although she said, 'That's probably just a bit of shock; I'll be fine.' And she tried to sit up again.

'Where the hell do you think you're going?' he said exasperatedly.

'Well, I can't stay here——'

'Of course you can, just do as you're told,' he ordered.

She subsided.

'What were you daydreaming about, in the middle of the night?' he asked after a while.

She was silent, her cheek resting on his shirt, his heart beating steadily beneath it.

'Sid?' He smoothed her hair gently.

'All sorts of things,' she said with an effort and closed her eyes on foolish tears. 'I'd rather not talk about it,' she added barely audibly.

She thought he sighed. 'This?' he said very quietly, and touched her face with his fingers.

'No, Mike,' she whispered. 'I've never let myself do that, not really.' And it was true that she'd refused to allow herself to make that great leap in her imagination to being his lover.

'All the same,' he said gently, 'it seems to be more than I can do to let you be sad and lonely—with a sore head as well.'

She moved her cheek. 'I'm fine really.'

'Well, maybe this will make you finer.' And he got up with her and carried her into his cabin and laid her on the double bed.

'Mike . . . ?' Her eyes were huge.

'No, I'm not going to do anything like that; relax, Sid—how many times have I told you that?'

'Quite a lot.' She bit her lip.

'What I had in mind was swapping beds with you tonight; this is much more comfortable, plus I can sit here——' he indicated the small armchair '—and read you nonsense stories until you go to sleep.'

She did relax a bit then. 'Oh! But you don't have to and I think you might be a bit too tall for my bunk.'

'I can sleep anywhere,' he said wryly. 'Don't go away.'

He came back some minutes later, with her book of Edward Lear and her pyjamas. 'Hop into these and I'll make us something to drink.'

She got up cautiously and changed into her pink tailored pyjamas, felt a bit dizzy so she stared at the bed, then, as she heard him coming back, slid beneath the covers.

This time he brought with him two steaming cups of cocoa. 'Warm enough now?'

'Yes. Look, thanks very much for all this,' she said shyly. 'I hate to be a nuisance.'

'As a matter of fact, in some respects, you couldn't be less of a nuisance if you tried.' He opened the book and his lips twitched. 'It's years since I've read this. I take it this bookmark is where you got up to the other night?'

'Yes.'

'Well, here goes; listen, prop yourself up a bit and drink your cocoa—I think it's supposed to help for shock—and in the meantime I shall start to declaim.'

He read well and after she'd finished her drink Sidonie slid back down and rested her cheek on her hand and listened with drowsy pleasure. Then her eyelids closed and, imperceptibly, she fell asleep. So she didn't hear him get up and stand beside the bed for a while as he gazed down at her, at the mass of her cornsilk hair curling on the pillow, the pale pink of her lips and the fine, faintly golden skin of her arms and neck. Nor did she hear him say, 'Though you may not realise it, my friend Sid, there are times when you remind of a thorny but sweet, wild, little rose—what *am* I going to do with you?'

The next morning she not only had a bump but a livid bruise just below her hairline, and a headache.

'Stay put,' Mike commanded when he came in just after she'd woken to check on her.

'But I can't stay in bed all day,' she protested.

'I'll bring you something for the headache and you'll stay in bed until it clears up—just do as you're told, Sidonie.'

She opened her mouth, read the determination in his eyes and said meekly instead, 'What kind of a day is it?'

'Overcast and it'll probably rain—you couldn't have chosen a better day for it.'

She subsided and half an hour later he brought her breakfast. Rain was indeed hammering on the deck. But despite her doubts about spending the day in bed it turned out to be a comfortable, homely day. They played Scrabble once her headache had cleared up, she had a long sleep after lunch, and as it still poured while the afternoon turned to a murky dusk he told her some more about his job, and the cottage he rented in rural England not far from where he worked, and the dog he owned and had to board out with friends whenever he came to Australia, to its utmost chagrin.

She said, 'Will you ever come back here to live, do you think?'

He shrugged. 'Probably.' And didn't sound as if he cared to enlarge at all.

She said no more but after dinner he let her get up and put a video on—they could get no television in this remote area—and it seemed perfectly natural when he sat down beside her on the settee and put his arm casually round her shoulder. Natural and friendly and she didn't realise that she looked particularly like a stray waif in her pink pyjamas with that dark bruise on her forehead. Nor when the movie, which was a thriller, got to a very exciting stage and she was watching with bated breath did it seem odd for him to look down at her wryly and kiss the top of her head lightly as he said, 'I don't know if this was a very good idea; you might have nightmares.'

She laughed and snuggled closer to him quite unconsciously. And that was how she stayed until the movie finished, when she came back to earth with a crash and realised it was the loveliest thing to be close to him as she was but she wasn't sure how it had happened or, even more particularly, why he had allowed it to happen. So she lifted her head and there was sheer consternation in her eyes but instead of moving her away or saying something to break the spell he hesitated, touched one finger to her parted lips then bent his head and kissed them.

'Sweet Sid,' he said a long time later, very quietly, 'I shouldn't have done that.'

'No...' She looked away confusedly, still bemused by the wonder of her first real kiss, because she'd never felt like this in her life before, although she'd had a few intimations of the sheer sensual wonder Mike Brennan aroused in her before she'd clamped down on those kind of thoughts. Now it was impossible, she discovered. Impossible to be unaware of the sensations in her own body and unaware of his, impossible not to think of him making love to her, touching her breasts, which felt tight and expectant, and not to think of touching herself to him with no clothes between them...

He drew her head back on to his shoulder. 'But now it is done—do you really regret it?'

'How could I?' she said huskily, which was true but she was also unable to think of anything else to say, yet she forced herself to make the effort. 'I didn't exactly fight you off so I'm as much to blame, I expect, if anything—if it shouldn't have been done...' She trailed off uncertainly.

'No.' He took her hand and fitted his fingers through hers. 'I'm afraid the blame's all mine.'

'When you say that...' she paused '...it's very hard to know what to think.'

'Well, tell me some of your thoughts on the subject,' he prompted and rubbed his chin on her hair.

'Mike...' she tried to gather the threads of her thoughts, which wasn't at all easy when all she wanted to do was bury herself against him and be held even closer '...it was true what I told you last night. I've never really let myself think about...this. There are probably two good reasons for that—I don't have the experience or that kind of imagination for it, or I didn't... And I knew...I'd only get more hurt if I did. That's one set of thoughts,' she said, and swallowed.

'Go on.' He pressed her fingers gently.

'And you made it so plain you didn't think of me in this way,' she said in a rush, 'that now I'm really confused.'

'Sid,' he said, rather bleakly, she thought, 'I was wrong. Your—charm has been growing on me. What overlaid it was the fact that nothing else I told you has changed.'

'That you're a lost cause, you mean?'

'That I'm the last person for a girl like you,' he said sombrely. 'You're right about what I do not being as dangerous as it sounds but it's not an easy occupation to live with either. Perhaps even more—fatal,' he said after a brief pause, 'to a stable relationship is that it expresses me perfectly. I don't like to be tied down. Even my dog knows that,' he added with considerable irony.

'Who's to say I would want to tie you down?' she said—the first words that came to mind but not spoken in any spirit of defiance, as he must have seen after casting her a frowning little glance.

'What do you mean?' he queried.

'Well,' she said, and the way she was concentrating showed in her eyes, 'I'm not exactly a conventional person myself.' Despite herself a faint smile touched her lips. 'I thought that may have been a bit obvious. So,' she sobered, 'well, I haven't suffered from what a lot of girls my age seem to suffer from—yet. Perhaps suffer is the wrong word,' she said quickly. 'They may be quite normal and I'm the odd one out—it's usually that way with me—but what I'm trying to say is that I don't have any maternal pangs, although I like kids; I haven't been plagued by any...visions of domestic bliss with a man, you included—that could even be a sure road to disaster for me; I haven't——'

'Sid, stop,' he said with a laugh.

'It's true!'

It was his turn to sober. 'It may be,' he said quietly, 'but they could still come. And I have to point out to you that you treat *Morning Mist* like a precious home.'

She bit her lip. 'It's still only a boat, though,' she said uncertainly after a moment of thought. 'And I think the home bit is in my heart,' she added with unconscious wisdom. 'I guess what I'm trying to say is, I can do without conventional homes, even conventional relationships.' She stopped and sighed.

He was silent for so long that she stirred at last and looked up at him. 'Mike?'

'Sid,' he said abruptly, 'does what happened with Karen mean nothing to you?'

'Do you mean,' she said slowly, 'that I should be afraid of what kind of man you are because of it? I'm not.'

'You should be,' he said roughly, then, 'Oh, hell,' and gathered her up into his arms. 'You're so bloody sane in things that really matter, you're so unpretentious and unlike every other woman I've known— there are some things I can't *help* loving about you. Not the least being that you're without the slightest artifice, you wouldn't know how to be sexy and come-hither if you tried, you're as delicate and pretty in your own way... as a wild rose, and it's like a breath of pure fresh air! But it can't *last*, not with me.' And his blue eyes were curiously tormented as he stared down at her.

Sidonie took a shaky breath and closed her eyes. 'Whatever you say, Mike,' she murmured. 'I... you see, I never thought it could—even begin——'

'Oh, it could begin all right,' he said into her hair.

'But...' She stopped. They both stopped as *Morning Mist* rocked violently. 'What was that?' she whispered.

He swore. 'They were predicting a southerly change, but for tomorrow; I think it's come in early.' He swore again and put her away from him.

'But we'll be all right here, won't we?' she said anxiously.

'No, we won't; we could end up on the beach if it gets strong enough.'

'But Mike, it's still raining and it's probably as black as pitch out there——'

'All the same we're going to have to move round the island, Sid. You see, it's so unprotected out there, which is why the Percys haven't got a great name in any kind of weather unless you're on the right side of the island. Now listen, we're going to have to do this by radar.' Another strong gust hit the boat. 'Will you get the set warmed up and tuned in? I'll get the anchor up.' He reached for his oilskin, his night-glasses, and disappeared up the ladder and the engine throbbed to life. But a few minutes later he was down again. 'We've got real problems, Sid,' he said tersely. 'Switch on the radio.'

'What?' she asked fearfully.

'Not us, but another yacht must have come in without us knowing. I shone the spotlight on it and it's already dragged anchor; by the look of it they can't start the motor or something's wrong and they're heading for the beach—thanks.' He took the microphone from her and said into it, '*Blue Bird*, *Blue Bird*, this is *Morning Mist*; we're anchored behind you, what's your problem? Over.'

'*Morning Mist*, *Blue Bird*,' a thankful voice gasped. 'We couldn't get the anchor up when it started to drag, the winch is playing up and in the panic we may have flattened the battery—we can't get her to start although I must have a bit of power if the radio's working, but—you wouldn't have a spare battery, would you, mate?'

Mike grimaced and thought briefly before he pressed his PTT button. 'Affirmative, *Blue Bird*. Look, I'll get as close to you as I can then bring it over by dinghy—unless you've got yours in the water?'

'We haven't but . . .' there was a hesitation during which a woman's panicky voice could be heard '. . . but we'll try and put it down.'

'Negative,' Mike said decisively, 'just try to stay put. If you've got a spare anchor put *it* down—just throw it over—and I'll come across. *Morning Mist* standing by.'

'Mike,' Sidonie whispered.

'Sid, look, you can do it,' he said firmly but gently. 'Just head her into the wind and try to hold her there. The rain's eased off so with the help of the spotlight you'll be able to see where you are, but, all the same, watch your depth sounder and radar like a hawk; if you get too close in you'll go aground. I know the wind sounds fierce but the water isn't that rough yet, and I'll be as quick as I can. But if I don't go they could end up on the beach or on the rocks in a splintered wreckage, and don't forget you've got your beloved Gardiner beneath you and plenty of power to cope with this. Plus I know you can do it.' And he kissed her briefly on the lips and hoisted himself up the ladder again.

Sidonie touched her fingers to her lips then reached for her oilskin.

Once she'd orientated herself and felt the power he'd spoken of through the throttle, she shed all her nerves for herself and *Morning Mist* and her greatest concern was for Mike. Because the wind was undoubtedly strengthening and the water getting increasingly turbulent and she watched the dinghy ploughing through it with her heart in her mouth as she held *Morning Mist* as close off *Blue Bird* as she dared to go. It had not been easy to lower the dinghy with the added weight of the battery in it. It wasn't easy to swivel the spotlight, which was mounted on the mast and remotely operated, so that she didn't blind him, but it was going to take a lot more than would be required of her to get back. And she found herself praying silently.

It took an hour to fix the winch, connect the new battery and reel both anchors in, the second of which had also started to drag. But with a sigh of relief she saw *Blue Bird* turn into the wind, and heard Mike on the radio... 'Sid, I'm coming back.'

'Romeo, Mike. Be careful.'

How he made it she didn't know. Several times she thought he would be swamped and when he got to *Morning Mist* she couldn't even leave the helm to help him. But finally, looking strained and soaked, he slid down beside her. 'Well done, kid,' he said briefly and took the wheel. 'Now for the next instalment of this drama—they're following us round. You should *always* carry spare batteries on a boat—but I didn't have the heart to tell him with his poor silly wife having hysterics.'

Sidonie grimaced. Then she said tentatively, 'She might be a good cook.'

Some of the tension drained from his expression and he put his arm round her and hugged her. 'Give me a good sailor and a mechanic any day.'

The northern anchorage of Middle Percy was relatively calm but finding it in the conditions was not. So that when they both finally stumbled down the ladder, secure in the knowledge that not only *Morning Mist* but *Blue Bird* was safe, Sidonie could barely stand.

'You poor kid,' Mike said and stripped her oilskin off, 'this probably hasn't done you any good at all.'

'I'll be all right. You're the one who's been humping batteries round and so on.' But her face was white and her bruise stood out lividly.

'I'm as tough as they come,' he said with a faint smile touching his lips. But he flexed his shoulders wearily and there were still the marks of strain etched in the lines and angles of his face.

Sidonie took a breath then noticed his hands again. 'Your poor hands,' she said softly. 'They're all grazed and bruised.'

He looked at them ruefully. 'We had to pull *Blue Bird's* second anchor up by hand. They'll heal—we make a good pair, Sid——' But he stopped and looked at her intently as she started to crumple from sheer exhaustion, the tension of the night finally claiming her. He took her in his arms. 'Let's go to bed, sweet Sid.'

'I'll—I'll sleep in my own bunk,' she managed to stammer.

'Like hell you will.' He picked her up and shouldered his way into the aft cabin. 'Now don't say a word,' he admonished, 'because I couldn't sleep if I knew you were all tense and wound up. I'll be back in a moment.' And he laid her on the bed and pulled the covers over her.

Five minutes later he came back and slid in beside her, and took her in his arms again.

'Mike...' Some foolish tears slid on to the pillow.

'Just go to sleep, Sid.' He stroked her hair. 'You're not alone and you've been braver tonight than any girl I know. Relax, kid...'

CHAPTER SEVEN

'RELAX, kid...'

Sidonie drifted awake with his words on her mind, and there was sunlight streaming through the portholes. She sighed—and started to remember as Mike's hand tightened on her waist, then his grip loosened.

She remembered falling asleep against him, and the warmth it had brought her. But she'd woken a couple of hours later and been attacked by anxiety, as if they were still trying to find their way around Middle Percy in a dark, stormy sea, and he'd cradled her to him and stroked her hair. She'd slept again, for hours, she judged from the angle of the sun, and was still lying softly against him.

'Sid?' he said drowsily.

'Yes, Mike?' She tried to breathe deeply to calm her suddenly racing heart.

But he muttered, 'Sweet Sid,' and pulled her closer, burying his face in the curve of her neck and shoulder. 'How do you feel now?'

'Fine.' She lifted a hand tentatively and rested it on his shoulder. 'What about you?'

'Fine.' There was a pause then he lifted his head and said with an effort, 'A little too fine in point of fact.' He stared into her eyes with a frown in his own. 'I don't suppose you know what I mean, so——'

'Mike——' she swallowed '—I'm not that naïve or whatever. Am I?'

127

His hand moved again on her waist and something flickered in the blue of his eyes that she couldn't decipher. 'All the same, this is——'

'Lovely,' she said very quietly and seriously.

His gaze wandered from her mouth to her eyes and he closed his own briefly. 'What I was going to say was—it's also when things get out of hand and one tends to lose one's head.'

She smiled faintly. 'I kept my head last night, and I don't mean during all that drama but... after you kissed me I thought, No, if this isn't meant to be, it's foolish to pretend otherwise—now I can't help wondering if I was wrong.' She moved her palm on his bare shoulder. 'When... if it happens between two people who move each other emotionally, even if there's no future for it, might it not have a kind of grace of its own?'

His lips moved but it was a moment before he spoke. 'Yes,' he said at last. 'I think it might even have a rather unique kind of grace with you, but it——'

'I know, you're worried it will induce all sorts of trauma in me and that I'll start to dream... all sorts of impossible dreams. I can't say that I won't but then the time for that not to happen to me to some degree is already past—and that's not your fault, Mike, it's just one of those things. There is one thing you might not understand about me, though. I couldn't bear to see you unhappy—that's why I was so upset about Karen, because of the darkness it brought to you. And so, when the time comes, I could no more try to tie you down than I could fly myself. Perhaps other women have said this to you.' She looked at him steadily. 'I can only mean it.'

'Oh, God.' He took a tortured breath. 'Sid, I'm not proof against much more of this.'

'Well, that's what I wondered, and hoped,' she whispered, her grey eyes suddenly soft, 'because neither am I...'

'You told me once you hadn't got to the stage of picturing yourself going to bed with me, Sid,' he said very gently. 'Only last night you said something similar.'

'Things can change,' she said in a suddenly shaky voice, because she got the awful feeling she was about to be repulsed, however gently, but then she discovered herself feeling stubborn. 'And if I were really honest, I suppose it's been *there* in my subconscious... But last night, when you said I wouldn't know how to be sexy and come-hither, I didn't really appreciate what you meant, so if you were trying to say——'

'Sid, I wasn't trying to say that you *aren't*——'

'That I'm not...desirable?'

'Let's not get bogged down in semantics,' he said with a wry little smile. 'Those things, that kind of innocence is very desirable—and that's one of the reasons why I'm...in this rather unenviable situation—but——' he stilled the movement she made '—whatever other faults I have, and you know them now as well as anyone, seducing virgins is something I don't—I shouldn't be doing.'

Sidonie looked into his eyes. 'Or is it that you really do think I'm a bit of a freak, Mike?'

He ran his hands through her hair with a grimace. 'Of course not—what do you mean anyway?'

'I may be a virgin but I'm quite capable of some things,' she said very quietly. 'I may have clamped down on some thoughts but I can't help thinking them now. I love being in your arms, for example. I get quite breathless sometimes just to watch you and I now long to feel your hands on my body—when you kissed me last night, it was like a revelation—so I'm a very normal girl in those respects even if I don't come across as one.'

'Sid——'

'No, Mike,' she said softly but with determination, 'don't treat me like a fool. This—if you were to make love to me it wouldn't be seducing a virgin, it would be what I want, even in the full knowledge that it can have no future and although it's the first time it's ever happened to me. Do you really think——' she brought her hands up rather shyly and placed them flat on his chest '—I'm such a child in all respects? I know I haven't told you this but after Peter, as well as suffering from a bit of a dent to my self-esteem, I became much more *aware*, and I sometimes yearned to experience what he had; I felt that there was this lack in me——'

'You also told me it wasn't the lack of a man in your life you worried about,' he said gently.

'Well, you just can't—put a man in your life to order, can you? That doesn't mean to say you don't think about it or understand the lack. *I* may have a lot of faults but what I'm trying to say is, do you really believe I'm some sort of emotionally retarded girl who has no idea of what I might be getting into? You do me an injustice if that's the case but it's up to you.'

'No,' he said after a very long time, 'God help me. Did you mean...like this?' And he undid her pyjama-top and laid it aside, framing her breasts then cupping them in his hands.

Sidonie trembled and was flooded with a sensation of pure pleasure.

'And this?' He slid her pyjama-bottoms down and caressed her waist and hips and said on a sudden breath, 'So small and so sweet, I can't help wondering if I would break you...'

'I don't think it's ever been known to happen,' she whispered.

'No, of course not. All the same, we'll need to take care and the way to do that is for you to tell me if I'm hurting you at all.'

'I will,' she promised. 'Could you...could you kiss me again, Mike? It did such astonishing things to me last night, you see.'

'Oh, Sid.' He pulled her very close and she felt the tremor that ran through his big frame. Then he lifted his head and stared down into her eyes with a little glint in his own. 'Of course. That's an excellent way to begin.'

And that's how we became lovers, dear diary, Sidonie said to the diary in her mind, many days later when it seemed important to keep the record straight... It must be hard for you to believe that I would do a thing like that. But it wasn't so hard to do at all, he made sure of that, although I guess you're wondering more about my motivation. I suppose I have to confess there was this hope in my heart that it wouldn't ever end, that I would be the one. There was also something else, though. And it was the thought that here was the only man I'd ever wanted to make love to me. I couldn't stop myself knowing either that with

Mike I could just be myself and that there'd be no awful need to be coy or pretend I was things I wasn't . . . I thought, It will never be more perfect for me so perhaps it will help me, strengthen me and make me into a better, more grown-up person—it's not that easy to say what I really thought, other than that . . . with Mike it just couldn't be a bad or negative thing for me. I also thought, dear diary, it might help him, might lighten the load . . .

'There's always a problem about these things,' Mike said as they prepared dinner that night, the night of the day they'd become lovers.

'These?' Sidonie looked up from the mushrooms she was peeling and chopping so carefully. All she wore was one of his shirts and a pair of panties.

'No, these situations,' he replied gravely.

'Oh, you mean us! What's that?'

'Well——' he took a sip of wine and regarded her with a wicked little glint in his eyes '—it's hard to be abstemious.'

Her lips curved although she said gravely, 'Thank you.'

'Would you have the same problem by any chance?'

'If you mean would I rather be doing other things than chopping up mushrooms——' she wrinkled her brow '—perhaps.'

'Would you care to enlighten me?' He glanced briefly over his shoulder at the veal he was sautéing and to which he would add a mushroom sauce.

She stopped chopping. 'I don't think I've got the words for it,' she said slowly. 'Other than to say that the—ambience of your suggestion or what you implied, if I have it correct, has filled me with a feeling of delicious anticipation. How does that sound?' she enquired with a mischievous twinkle.

'Sounds like my essential Sid,' he drawled. 'Never really lost for a word. Or two. It also makes it even harder to concentrate on this meal, however.' His gaze rested on the open V of his shirt where the skin between her breasts was pearly then tantalisingly shadowed as she moved slightly beneath his scrutiny. Then it roamed to her loose, riotiously curling hair and came to rest again on the tip of her tongue as she concentrated fiercely on the last mushroom, and his eyes softened.

'There,' she said triumphantly but as she looked up a delicate blush tinged her cheeks.

'Sweet Sid,' he said gently, 'I shall have to try not to embarrass you.'

'I might . . . I might get more used to it,' she said, clasping her hands together urgently. 'It's all so new, you see.'

'But not unpleasant, I hope? Now you've had time to reflect upon it?'

'Oh, no,' she said fervently. 'It was—you were—I was right not to have too many preconceived ideas about it, I think. But then again it could just be that you're—so good at it.' She reached for her wine and sipped it thoughtfully.

His lips twisted and he turned to the veal, turned it over and gazed absently down at it. 'If that's so, you have to take some of the credit for it. And before I wreck this meal——' he turned back to her and eyed her humorously '—I think we should change the subject.'

Sidonie agreed rather heartily that they should.

But after dinner and after they'd done the dishes together he said softly, 'Come here.'

She went and curled up in his lap.

'Feeling better?'

She looked up into his eyes. 'I wasn't feeling—bad.'

'Just a little constrained?' he suggested.

'Well——' she bit her lip '—a little overwhelmed perhaps. But not *sorry* or anything like that,' she said hastily. 'Don't for one minute think that.'

He undid the buttons of the shirt and slid his hand beneath it. She trembled then quietened as his fingers roamed over her skin, circling her breasts then stroking her back and the swell of her hips.

Until finally she said, in a grave, deep little voice, 'That's so nice, Mike.'

'It is for me too. In fact making love to you, Sid, is one of the nicest things I've ever done.'

'I didn't think——' she stopped then made herself go on '—that I had the kind of body men would appreciate.'

'I gathered that but men can be quite discerning, you know. They can appreciate high, tender little breasts, skin like alabaster, lips like the palest pink coral and hips that are jaunty and as rounded as two perfect peaches.' He moved his hand below the elastic of her panties.

Although she blushed, she laughed quietly too. 'You're waxing lyrical, Mr Brennan. I don't know whether I ought to believe you.'

'Believe me, Sid. You're delicately, tantalisingly and fascinatingly fashioned.'

'So are you.' She grimaced wryly. 'I mean to say, I love the way you're put together—which is strong and rugged and seems to be like a haven to me, that is. I'm sorry I can't be more specific—oh, dear, I'm getting into a tangle, aren't I?' she said awkwardly. 'Is this kind of constraint, as you put it, normal?' she asked directly then. 'I was so sure I wouldn't have to be coy or anything like that.'

'Perfectly. And very appropriate for a girl who was a virgin less than twenty-four hours ago. Nor are you being coy; I don't think you could anyway.' He paused and she looked up at him, not sure whether he was teasing her, but his eyes as their gazes locked were serious. 'Men are a bit different, though, Sid. Once they embark on this, it's very hard to be constrained. Which means to say——' his eyes danced suddenly a bit, she thought '—that I'm now fascinated by every part of you, that I'm likely to be stricken with desire for you at the oddest times and, well, that's the nature of the beast unfortunately. I hope you'll not mind excessively and even see your way clear to take pity on me from time to time.'

He was to demonstrate this to her a day or so later...

'Is that a fact?' he said gravely to her one afternoon when she'd been discoursing knowledgeably on the subject of motorbikes—Eglis, Ducatis and the like. 'I can't imagine you all dressed up in black leather.'

'Oh, I don't think I'd like to drive them!'

'Just tune them? I'm relieved to hear you say so,' he murmured. They were sitting on the back deck, he was actually lounging on it, his head propped in his hand, and she was sitting cross-legged eating an orange, wearing shorts and her blue and white spotted blouse. 'As a matter of fact I can imagine you wearing—not much at all, however.'

Sidonie looked up from the last segment of her orange and discovered that he was watching her in a curiously heavy-lidded way.

'Mike,' she said with a tremor in her voice, 'do you mean now?'

A wicked little glint of amusement lit his eyes. 'I'm afraid so—I did warn you that this was liable to happen although of course I apologise for the inconvenience.'

She had to smile but then frowned. 'Is... is there something about me eating an orange...?' She found herself unable to go on.

'Definitely,' he agreed. 'Particularly when it's laced with hearing you talk about a 1000cc V twin Egli Vincent capable of doing a hundred and forty miles an hour—the mixture seems to be irresistibly seductive.'

Sidonie raised an eyebrow. 'Are you sure you're not simply thinking of a way to make me stop talking?'

He laughed. 'You can talk all you like so long as you take me to bed quite soon as well.'

But she was curiously lost for words when he laid her on his bed and took her clothes off item by item as if he was truly fascinated by her small, slim body.

Dear diary... I had no idea it would be the way it was. That he could be so sweet and funny—and even patient, I suspect, while I adjusted to it. Which took a bit of adjusting, I have to tell you, not so much him making love to me but the way everything was different, the way he was fascinated by every part of me, or seemed to be, the way everything we did from then on was...coloured by our sleeping together. And when I got more used to it, to him touching me, holding

ne, saying things to me when we were far removed
rom being in bed, it started to come more naturally
o me too—I probably was terrifically clumsy at it at
irst but he never seemed to mind. As a matter of fact
I got the impression he liked it but I might have been
wrong. Then there was the way he made love to me...

Mike?' she said a few days later.

'Sidonie?'

'Mike,' her voice shook, 'something incredible
seems to be happening to me.'

'Tell me,' he said very quietly, holding her while
his body moved on hers.

'It's like—it's like nothing else that has ever happened to me. It's like waves flowing up through me
that are so nice but although I've had a sort of
presentiment before... of them, this time...
Oh——' She closed her eyes and arched her body
against him. 'Oh, Mike, don't let me go...' she
pleaded.

'It's happening to me too, Sid,' he said very quietly
and reassuringly but his arms tightened about her and
their bodies moved together until they reached a final
crescendo.

A long time later when he still held her closely in
his arms and was smoothing the damp tangle of her
hair and watching her exhausted but radiant face she
whispered, 'I did it!'

'And beautifully.'

'I was beginning to wonder——'

He put a finger to her lips. 'I told you it was only
a matter of time.'

'Well, yes, I know but one can't help worrying, I
mean, one reads things and—wonders, you see.'

He smiled wryly down at her. 'What one should really do is take the advice of one's elders.'

She smiled back at him, her eyes alight with love and a little impish glint. 'I know but I have this enquiring mind. It's a great cross to bear sometimes. But I'll tell you what it tells me, and I'd be surprised if I were wrong in this. It tells me,' she said and slid her arms around his shoulders, 'that what you do to me beforehand is the secret to it all.'

'Not entirely,' he said gravely.

'Not?' She opened her eyes at him.

'Well, in the sense that you have to like what I do to you in the first place.'

She sighed and laughed. 'Who wouldn't?' Then she sobered. 'I have to thank you——'

'No, please——'

'Yes, I do and I'm quite determined so you might as well listen, Mike Brennan. Because you see, when I made the decision to do this, I was extremely ignorant of a lot of aspects of it, and I'm sure that showed—I mean, all I really knew was...that it seemed right to do it, and that I loved being in your arms and it didn't frighten me at all...what might come, so to speak.'

His lips twisted. 'Do you think I didn't know that, Sid?'

'Oh.' She looked momentarily downcast but recovered. 'But did you know that once it was done I felt a little bit inadequate? As well as shy and verbally clumsy and a few other things,' she said ruefully.

She felt him jolt with laughter but he said gently, 'I'm afraid to say I did, Sid. I tried to tell you it was perfectly normal, especially for someone like you.'

'So you did, but what really helped was the way you made me feel—as if *you* really wanted me——'

'I did and I do.'

'Anyway—oh——' she looked into his eyes '—I think I'll just say thanks. I always did talk too much.' And she buried her face in his shoulder suddenly. This, today, and all the other days, is the nicest thing that's ever happened to me,' she continued in a gruff, muffled little voice, however. 'I just wanted you to know in case my...constraint seemed like something else. And, whatever happens, nothing can change it.'

He was silent for a long time then he tilted her face and kissed her. But there was a spark of something oddly sombre in his eyes.

During all this the weather remained unsettled so they were forced to spend an extended stay at the Percy Islands but finally the day dawned when they felt the sunshine might not be a false alarm and they set sail for Island Head Creek on the mainland.

'What's there?' Sidonie asked excitedly, intoxicated by the breeze in the sails and the shush of their bow wave.

Mike grimaced. 'Nothing.'

'Nothing?'

'Well, other than the army.'

Her eyes widened. 'What do you mean?'

He laughed at her expression. 'The whole Shoalwater Bay area is an army training reserve which is not conducive to it being a residential area, apart from the fact that it's miles away from anywhere, anyway.'

'Do you mean it's a sort of firing range?'

'From time to time.'

'Why are we going there, Mike?'

'They let you know well in advance if you shouldn'
be there; we'll be quite safe.' He took her hand. 'There
are two great natural harbours on this part of the
coast—Island Head Creek and Pancake Creek, which
is south of Gladstone. They're both virtually uninhabited and they abound with fish, crabs and oysters
as well as having a sort of wild beauty of their own.
I think you'll like Island Head.'

It was to occur to Sidonie that she would like the
far side of the moon, if they were there together.

They spent two days at Island Head Creek, which
despite it being called a creek was a large body of
sheltered water fringed with white beaches or, in some
spots, bush-clad, rocky ridges. They were unable to
explore the ridges because of the dangers of unex-
ploded shells, but it was off a lovely beach that her
swimming lessons commenced . . .

'Mike, I might not be the kind of person who takes
naturally to swimming——'

'Nonsense—no one takes naturally to it anyway.
Just do as you're told, Sid, and stop talking otherwise
you'll get a mouthful of water.'

'But . . .' She sank and came up spluttering.

'I told you,' he said with a grin.

'Mike, I can't even stand here,' she protested and
clung to him like a wet monkey. She was also wearing
her red bikini—a mistake, she conceded to herself,
since it seemed not to have lost its association with
another watery, traumatic occasion.

'Ah, but I can,' he said, 'and do you honestly think
I would stand by and let you drown, Sid?'

'No,' she said, but crossly, 'just let me make a fool
of myself and swallow half of Island Head Creek!'

'Not if you do as you're told,' he repeated patiently.

She made a disgusted sound then took a deep breath but stopped halfway through. 'You're determined to do this, aren't you, Mike?'

'I am,' he replied placidly.

'You really don't have to worry about me falling into a pond and drowning,' she said bitterly.

'No, I won't, because by the time you've calmed down and let me show you a few things you'll be well on your way to swimming.'

'Don't count on it,' she warned darkly but he unwound her arms, kissed her wet cheek and placed her on her back in the water with his hand underneath her waist.

'I think I can do it,' an amazed Sidonie was heard to say some time later.

'Told you so,' her mentor said brazenly and scooped her up in his arms. 'What you can do now is float. Tomorrow I'll show you how to breathe.'

It was not long afterwards when they were back aboard *Morning Mist* that he removed her wet bikini, dried her fresh body and placed her naked on the bed, saying casually, 'Still cross with me, Miss Hill?'

Sidonie considered, refusing to allow the smile that wanted to curve her lips to surface. 'You're a very dictatorial, even hard person sometimes, Mike,' she said neutrally.

'So I've been told.' He stripped off his own togs, lay down beside her and started to stroke her body until her nipples unfurled and she began to tremble with desire.

She sighed and moved into his arms. 'It's also harc to stay cross with you when you do that, not that I was, really.'

'Good——'

'Mike——' she sat up suddenly '—can I ask you something?'

He grimaced and folded his arms behind his head. 'Fire away.'

'I didn't——' she hesitated '—I had the impression that... what happened between men and women would be a lot more *dramatic* than it really is.'

His eyes danced with sudden devilry. 'Would you like us to be dramatic, Sid? I take it you mean something like me dragging you by the hair off to my cave—that sort of thing?' There was a teasing query in his eyes now.

'Oh, no.' She shivered. 'I don't think I'd like that at all.' She paused and looked thoughtful.

'So what did you mean?'

'I'm not really sure,' she said slowly. 'But you often read about it as being full of deep, dark, brooding passion and—things like that. Getting carried away on a *blaze* of sensuality, against your will kind of thing. Looking into some man's dark eyes across a room and being set on fire——'

'Do you mean——' he touched one of her pale pink velvety nipples '—that I don't set you on fire, Sid?'

She trembled. 'No—yes, you do,' she said with an effort.

'I wonder.' He looked up at her with a faintly narrowed look.

'What do you mean?' she asked after a moment.

'Nothing——'

'No, you can tell me,' she said earnestly. 'Because I'll be perfectly honest and say that I sometimes wonder whether for you I'm a bit like fish and chips as opposed to——' she gestured '—Dover sole. I mean to say,' she added, 'fish and chips are nice and...homely, I guess, but Dover sole is—special.'

For a moment his expression was entirely quizzical. Then he said, 'For me, you *are* special, so banish the thought of fish and chips from your mind—and do you intend to talk to me and tantalise me at the same time for much longer?' He brought his hands down and put them about her waist. 'Because if so, my lovely water sprite, I will have a problem.' And he moved his hands up to cup her breasts.

'Mike, I can't think when you do that,' she murmured.

'I know,' he said softly and drew her down so he could tease her nipples with his tongue. 'Better still, you can't talk.'

'No,' she conceded a little helplessly. 'Well, not nearly as effectively as if I were otherwise engaged. In fact you've quite managed to distract my thoughts.'

'Good,' he murmured and continued paying exquisite attention to her breasts until she was finally struck speechless. Then he laid her on her back and slid his hand between her thighs and caressed the most intimate part of her with a touch so gentle she barely felt it, yet it caused that lovely tide to start to rise in her body and she said his name and opened her arms to him.

'Sweet Sid,' he said barely audibly, as he lowered his weight on to her and entered her warm, arching body, 'believe me, this is pure Dover sole.'

But she found herself wondering later whether that was true, or whether he'd subtly deflected her. And she also found herself wondering what he'd meant when he'd said that he wondered if he set her on fire. How can he doubt it? she asked herself, and jumped as she felt his hand on her knee.

She was sitting cross-legged with her chin in her hands at the top of the ladder that led down to the cabin, watching the sun set and thinking all these serious thoughts; he was standing, she discovered, on the bottom rung so that his head was level with her waist, and he could have been there for ages, so engrossed had she been.

'You're lost in thought, Sid. Want to tell me?'

She put her hands on his shoulders and smiled faintly. 'No.'

'Now you've really got me worried—have I done something wrong?'

She looked into his eyes, observed the wicked little glint, and strove for a light note. 'I feel it in me at this moment in time to—preserve a mysterious silence.' She slid her fingers through his hair and added, 'I sometimes miss your red bandanna, Mike.'

He grimaced. 'Why?'

'I don't know. Perhaps it was a symbol that you were more in my league.' She stopped and bit her lip.

If he observed it he didn't comment but pointed out to her that she'd thoroughly mistrusted both him and his red bandanna at one stage.

She had to laugh. 'Well...'

'Admit it, Sid. You even alerted the local police, after all.'

'So I did—well, it didn't actually happen quite like that,' she protested, then shrugged delicately. 'And now look what's happened to me. They'd all be *so* amazed. I doubt if I would have the courage to ever set foot in Airlie Beach again.'

He said gently, 'If they could see you now they'd think you were a sight for sore eyes. You've blossomed into something warm, golden and lovely.'

Sidonie looked down into his blue eyes and was possessed of a flood of feeling that shook her to the core. She'd been through the stages of liking Mike, of loving him in an almost abstract way, of wanting to see him happy above all and feeling infinitely safe with him. Then she'd discovered the joy of being his lover as he'd initiated her so carefully and patiently, but now she was suddenly possessed of something far deeper and she wondered if this was what being a woman was all about, if she'd finally come to all the knowledge, the joy and the pain that went with the estate. Because, at the same time as she felt an astonishing tenderness for Mike Brennan that was like a physical sensation and caused her breasts to tingle and her insides to melt, she also felt hauntingly sad because one day she was going to have to let him go. And she knew that her body was going to crave him as much as her mind, that she would never be able to separate the effect he had on her again.

And in an almost reflexive gesture she put her hands around the back of his head and cradled it to her breasts. Then she released him just as suddenly and said with a wry little smile, 'Am I getting a cooking lesson tonight?'

'If you want—Sid . . .' he hesitated briefly then put his hands on her waist and swung her down into the cabin '. . . what was that about?'

'Nothing, Mike.' She took his hand and threaded her fingers through his at the same time as she said gaily, 'Lead on, Mr Master Chef. In point of fact I'm starving. Is that what swimming does to you?'

But things changed after that day.

Not dramatically and not when they were making love but at other times they were both quieter, Sidonie thought, and said to herself, Well, it has to end, doesn't it? And swallowed with sudden fright.

They also had a blazing row.

It all began quite innocently...

'So this is Rosslyn Bay!' she said as *Morning Mist* slid into a man-made harbour beneath a towering inverted pear-shaped rock.

'Uh-huh.' Mike was at the wheel. 'Gateway to the Capricorn Coast, you might say. Great Keppel is not far away seaward, Rockhampton not far away inland, and that's the township of Yeppoon you can see. But the only reason most people come into Rosslyn Bay is to refuel and take on water. And use the laundromat.'

Sidonie wrinkled her nose. 'You don't like it.'

'I guess it's a reminder that the trip—that we're getting closer to civilisation now,' he amended. 'Plus it's not the most aesthetically appealing place I've been to—hell,' he added.

She raised an eyebrow at him.

'There are at least five boats lined up waiting to refuel; this will take hours. We'll have to spend the night here.'

'Is that a problem?'

'No, you can anchor over there.'

'Well, I'll tell you what,' she said brightly, 'while you're waiting to refuel, why don't I try out this famous laundromat? Our towels and sheets need a good wash.'

He glanced at her a shade wickedly, she thought but she tried to remain nonchalant. 'You could be right,' he said gravely.

'Is there anywhere you could drop me off?'

'Certainly, that jetty there. But the laundromat is a bit of a walk.'

Sidonie jumped up. 'I don't mind. Just show me the general direction.'

'Have you ever used a laundromat before?'

'Hundreds of times,' she assured him, adding indignantly, 'I'm not really some babe in the woods, Mike.'

'Not quite,' he agreed. 'Do you know that little blue jar in the galley cupboard where the cups and saucers are?'

'Yes.'

'You'll find it chock-a-block with coins of the designation so beloved by laundromats.'

'What a good idea!'

'I'm full of 'em,' he agreed.

'And sometimes you're so modest——' she patted him on the head '—it's incredible.'

He took one hand off the wheel and pulled her into his lap. 'Don't do anything I wouldn't while you're ashore, Miss Hill.'

She looked up into his eyes, saw how they teased and went limp with love. 'I won't,' she promised because for once she couldn't think of anything else to say.

But she did, quite unwittingly, and she had no presentiment as she strode out jauntily from the jetty with her beloved hat upon her head to protect her from the sun and a bag of laundry swinging in her hand.

There were only two other people in the laundromat—a pretty dark girl of about nineteen and her baby in a pram. But although she was pretty the girl's eyes were swollen and red-rimmed as she sorted through a mountain of nappies and baby clothes, and she responded to Sidonie's cheerful greeting with only a watery smile. Moreover, it wasn't long before she sat down on the bench, dropped her head into her hands and began to sob pitifully. The baby immediately started to wail in sympathy.

'Oh, dear,' Sidonie said worriedly and she picked the baby up, sat down beside the girl and tried to comfort them both.

It finally came out, a long, sad story about the trials of being an unmarried mother, how it was so hard to cope, how lonely she was even though she was living with her parents, how their unspoken disapproval came through, how she sometimes, although they had a perfectly good washing machine at home, came down here just to get *away* . . . How she still loved the father of her baby despite his defection.

Sidonie shook her head and marvelled inwardly. But apparently just being able to unburden herself to a sympathetic stranger helped because finally the girl dried her tears, and together they transferred loads of washing to the driers and sorted it and folded it as it came out, in quite a spirit of companionship. Because there were only three, slow driers, though, Sidonie's washing was last to go in and still drying when Pauline—they'd exchanged names—was ready to go with several large bags balanced precariously on the top of the pram hood.

'Have you got far to go?' Sidonie asked.

'About a mile up the road.'

Sidonie glanced at the drier and made a decision. 'I'll walk up with you, then; mine is still going to take ages, I think. Here, let me carry a bag.'

But it was at least a mile up the main Yeppoon road then half a mile down a side one—and she'd left her hat in the laundromat, Sidonie realised. Not that she minded; the sun was sinking and was losing its strength and Pauline pressed her to come in and have a cup of tea. But belatedly Sidonie thought of Mike, who might be wondering what had happened to her, so she declined but she took note of the address and suggested they might become pen-pals. The other girl was so grateful, Sidonie wished she could do more, and had this on her mind as she walked back the way they'd come. She was also thinking that Rosslyn Bay was a lonely sort of place to be stranded with a baby— it was really nothing more than a fishing village—and got the fright of her life when a police car skidded to a halt beside her and a burly constable enquired whether she might be Sidonie Hill.

'Yes, yes,' she breathed, immediately imagining that some terrible accident had befallen Mike. 'What's happened?'

The constable reached resignedly for his radio. 'Nothing, love. Your boyfriend's just doing his nut. Convinced you got kidnapped 'cause he reckons you wouldn't have gone anywhere willingly without your hat.' And he cast Sidonie a speaking look.

'How d-dare you?' Sidonie's voice quivered with anger. 'How dare you say things like that to me in front of a whole lot of people?'

They were back on *Morning Mist*; she'd just scrambled off the dinghy and stood on the back deck with her hands on her hips, her hat on her head. 'Of all the——'

'They were all too true,' he replied cuttingly as he came up the ladder himself and threw the bag of laundry on the deck. 'You were gone for bloody *hours*. What do you think I should have done? I checked the shops, I checked anywhere you might legitimately be expected to go—there are not a lot of places one *can* go in Rosslyn Bay—and to all intents and purposes you had vanished into thin air.'

'But I *hadn't*——'

'And we can continue this discussion down below,' he said curtly and simply picked her up and carried her there.

Sidonie kicked and fought on the way down, as angry as she could ever recall being, but to no avail. She also said when he finally set her on her feet, 'I *hate* you, Mike Brennan! *All* I was doing was a good turn, and it was *so* little, for some poor girl——'

'Well, the next time you get carried away doing good deeds, just let me know in advance.' He stared at her, his eyes still smouldering, his mouth set in a hard line, then he turned away abruptly and reached for a bottle of Scotch.

Sidonie watched him in silence as he poured a drink. Then she said tautly, 'I never thought you would be the kind of person to make so much out of a simple misunderstanding, Mike. I'm...I have to confess I'm disappointed in you.'

'*Disappointed*,' he ground out and banged a second glass on to the counter. 'What you don't understand is that girls do get picked up and whisked away and

God knows what else. So to blithely walk miles away and leave your belongings, your precious damned *hat* behind,' he said witheringly, 'would look suspicious to anyone! To *me*,' he stressed the word, 'who knows only too well how much trouble you can get yourself into without even trying—it certainly looked that way,' he finished furiously.

Sidonie pursed her lips and decided to ignore that taunt. 'Are you not just a little embarrassed about over-reacting, Mike? Although the police were pretty understanding, I thought. Especially when you started to abuse me.'

'Embarrassed!' he marvelled. 'You're damn right.' He took a sip of straight Scotch and breathed exasperatedly. 'You'd try the patience of a saint, Sidonie.'

'If that's the case, you don't have to put up with me, Mike. I can go any time, you know,' she said proudly.

He only smiled but it was a tigerish, cynical little smile and he glanced around expressively as if to say, Where exactly do you plan to go, friend Sid?

Sidonie suddenly experienced the sensation of being dangerously overwrought, as if this couldn't—or shouldn't—be happening to her. And two tears sparkled on her lashes and brimmed over.

Mike stared at her then said in a suddenly goaded sort of voice, 'Come here, Sid.'

'No, Mike.' She sniffed and scrubbed her eyes with her wrists. 'Not until you apologise——'

'What the hell have I got to apologise for?' he demanded.

'For treating me the way you did. For making such a fool of me in front of... the whole town! I tried to apologise and explain what had happened. I tried to tell you *why* it had all happened but you wouldn't listen—well, I'm not going to listen now.' And she stood straight and stern in her yellow T-shirt and blue shorts, her hat still on her head, and didn't bother to scrub the tears away any more. 'I feel extremely misused, if you must know, and quite determined not to give in to your overbearing tactics, which are nothing short of bullying of the highest order to my mind.'

For a moment his expression defied description then he deliberately relaxed. 'All right,' he drawled, 'I apologise. Would you care to share a drink with me?'

She stared at him. 'I don't think you really mean that, Mike——'

'Oh, for God's sake!' He came round the counter and picked her up and sat her on it. He also removed her hat, murmuring that it had done enough damage for one day. Then he said gravely, 'I'm sorry, Sid. I genuinely got a fright; I couldn't for the life of me imagine where you might have gone and . . . well, the rest you know. But you have to admit it was pretty thoughtless to wander off like that, in a strange place.'

'I suppose so,' she conceded. 'But she was just so miserable, you see. And she had this *sweet* baby— I'm going to write to her. Just pen-pal sort of thing; it can only help, don't you think?'

'Well, so long as she doesn't turn up on your doorstep one day complete with sweet baby—uh—no, only teasing,' he said ruefully. 'Am I forgiven?'

Sidonie considered then she said, 'Yes. Provided, though——'

'I might have known there would be a proviso,' he said with an ironic little smile.

'That you stop treating me as if I can't take care of myself.'

'Can you?' He said it almost in a reflexive gesture, she thought, then smiled, but drily, as he added, 'OK. Should we kiss and make up?'

'If you want to——'

'I do. Don't you?' He raised a quizzical eyebrow at her.

'Why do I get the feeling I'm being patronised?' she asked more of herself, as if speaking her thoughts aloud.

'I wouldn't dream of patronising you, Sid,' he replied, however, and drew his hands lightly down her arms. 'You're quite—terrifying,' he added innocently, 'when you get all haughty and proud and climb on to your high horse. For basically a slip of a girl, you grow amazingly in stature.'

'Well, now I know you are patronising me, Mike Brennan——'

'And I can see there's only one way around this one,' he broke in wryly and, taking her in his arms, began to kiss her without further ado.

Later, in the dark, as she lay beside him holding his hand, sated and drowsy and feeling worshipped from the tips of her toes to the crown of her curly head, he said very quietly, 'Still feeling misused, Sid?'

She sighed and turned into his arms. 'No. It's impossible. Although I suspect I should.'

He laughed. 'What say we leave Rosslyn Bay very early in the morning and try our luck at Pancake Creek? I can't think of any disasters that might befall us there.'

'All right.' She snuggled closer to him and was not to know that Pancake Creek would provide the biggest disaster of all, from her point of view.

CHAPTER EIGHT

DEAR diary, it was on the way to Pancake Creek that I got the feeling I was on a runaway train. I think what happened at Rosslyn Bay precipitated it and I knew we both had it on our minds as we sailed south; I could almost hear him saying to himself, What the hell am I going to do with you, Sid? No, not quite as he did say it to me once, not angrily but perhaps with a different and genuine concern, a sense of different responsibility, because, of course, I couldn't hide how I felt ... I couldn't be half-hearted about loving him although I tried not to make it too obvious. So what were we going to do? That was on our minds and we couldn't help it creeping into our conversation—then two things came up...

'Have you got a permanent berth at Tin Can Bay, Mike?'

'Yes—what brought that to mind, Sid?'

They were about an hour out of Pancake Creek and motoring because the sea was dead calm, its surface like a mirror for the blue sky above, and there was not a breath of breeze.

Sidonie patted the wooden deck she was sitting on, patiently splicing a rope. 'It's just hard to think of *Morning Mist*——' she squinted up at the bare mast and halyards '—being laid up for months and months.'

'Yes,' he said, 'it's not the best solution but about the only one. Still, I've had an extra month off this time so I can't complain.'

'When are you due back?' she asked quite naturally.

'In two weeks.'

Two weeks—she repeated it in her mind and felt as if a hand was squeezing her heart suddenly, and all her naturalness deserted her. 'So,' she said with an effort, 'do you think you'll keep her? I mean, I gathered that you'd had a series of boats from what they told me in Airlie Beach.'

He glanced at her briefly. 'Mmm. I worked my way up to *Morning Mist*, you might say, by buying a couple of second-hand yachts and doing them up and selling them on.'

'You wouldn't . . . sell her on, though, would you?' To her consternation she was unable to keep the anxiety out of her voice and eyes.

'No. This is it.'

She relaxed a little.

'Why, Sid?' he queried quietly.

'I . . . just like to think of you two together, that's all,' she said awkwardly.

'The perfect mistress,' he said drily after a time. 'I can pack her up and put her away any time I want.'

Sidonie digested the tinge of self-directed cynicism behind his words and got up and showed him the rope. 'There, perfectly spliced anyway. That's one thing you didn't have to teach me, Mike——' She stopped abruptly.

'Sid——'

No, Mike, please don't,' she whispered. 'Let's talk about something else. Did you know, for example, that Captain Cook named Bustard Head behind which

lies Pancake Creek in 1770? And he so named it because they shot a fowl there that was the best bird
they'd eaten since leaving home.'

He was silent for a moment, watching her carefully, then he said, 'You're a mine of information,
Miss Hill.'

'I've been reading his diary in your *Cruising the
Curtis Coast* book,' she replied gaily. 'I wondered if
they had pancakes for breakfast one day round about
that time but I can't find any reference to it.'

He smiled absently then his gaze narrowed on the
southern horizon. 'There's that change they forecast.
We might be stuck with pancakes for breakfast for a
few days, Sid.'

She scanned the horizon and saw the build-up of
clouds. 'Oh.'

He took her hand and pulled her down beside him.
All he wore was a pair of shorts and he was tanned
nearly mahogany all over apart from where his shorts
covered so that by contrast her own golden glow
looked pale, and she felt small next to his smoothly
muscled bulk and long, powerful legs. Not that she
minded, normally. Somehow or other he contrived to
make her slender body, her waist, which he could
nearly span with his hands, her narrow hands and feet
feel gloriously feminine, something she'd never really
felt before. But today, at that moment, all she felt was
small and worried.

'Don't look like that,' he said, linking his arms
loosely round her. 'It won't be like all the drama we
had at Middle Percy or the storm we got into getting
there. Pancake is as protected as Island Head. All you
get is a slight roll in a northerly.'

She leant her cheek on his shoulder and said softly, 'Middle Percy was special, though.' And immediately winced inwardly. Why do I keep *saying* these things?

'Yes.' He rested his chin on her head but said no more as the Gardiner beneath them maintained its even, steady beat and carried them on.

But there was a surprise waiting for them at Pancake Creek—*Moonshine*, riding gently on her anchor in the broad placid reach of the creek.

'Bloody hell!' Mike swore. 'I might have known.'

'Oh, no,' Sidonie said. 'I wonder if Karen's with him?'

'Someone's with him,' Mike said coldly, and stopped.

'Who is it? I don't think I recognise her; it doesn't look like Karen, does it?'

Mike said nothing for more than a minute during which he also turned around and examined what he could see of the sky behind Bustard Head and all around; and he had never looked more Red Indian and totally, impassively withdrawn as he did it, Sidonie thought and caught her breath. Then he said, 'It's his sister.'

Sidonie gasped then followed the track his gaze had taken around the sky. 'Mike,' she said involuntarily, 'we can't go out in this. It's coming really fast——'

'Of course we can't; I wasn't going to suggest it,' he said drily.

But you thought it for a moment, Sidonie said to herself. Will it be that painful to see Tim Molloy's sister again? she also wondered with a strange, sick feeling. 'He might not want to have anything to do with you...with us,' she said, pressing her palms together urgently.

'Is that why he's waving at us like a threshing machine?' Mike suggested with irony.

'But this could be very awkward,' she said slowly.
Tim was indeed waving enthusiastically although the
girl behind him had so far not made any gesture.

'No, it won't,' Mike said, bringing the throttle back
to neutral as he positioned *Morning Mist* behind
Moonshine, and pressing a button so that the anchor
fell into the water with a splash and the chain rattled
out after it. 'Merely inescapable if I know my friend
Tim. He's quite unsquashable. Anyway, Sid,' he said,
turning to look directly into her eyes, 'it was all over
years ago whatever Tim may have intimated to you
to the contrary. Helen is married now and I'm not
manfully concealing a broken heart so don't *you* start
getting yourself into a tangle...'

But Helen Cook née Molloy was no longer married,
except technically, as it turned out, and she was one
of the most seriously beautiful women Sidonie had
ever seen.

Tall and lithe, she had a graceful figure, glorious
long hair the colour Titian would have sold his soul
for, beautiful hazel eyes beneath strongly marked
brows, a wide, lovely but hauntingly sad mouth and
a quietly diffident air that made you want to make
her smile...

It was also obvious after only a few minutes in her
company that she couldn't have been less like Karen
if she tried. *Why*? Sidonie found herself wondering
throughout that confused evening. She's not only
lovely but so nice, *why* didn't they make it, her and
Mike? She would be perfect for him...

But before she got to that stage she had to contend with Tim, who had his dinghy in the water almost as soon as they'd anchored and came zooming over.

'Great to see you folks!' he called as he heaved his teddy-bear bulk up the back ladder. 'Wondered if we might catch up with you somewhere!'

Sidonie thought Mike sighed before he said gently, 'Good to see you too, mate. I take it you bear me no hard feelings?'

'Well, the less said about that the better, but she was a right bitch so, although it's hard to concede you actually did me a good turn . . .' he smiled ruefully '. . . in point of fact you did. And how's my little friend Sid?' he added playfully and chucked her under the chin.

'Fine, Tim!'

'You look it too. Guess what?' He turned to Mike ingenuously. 'I've got Helen with me. Flew her up to Hamilton after I had to fly Karen almost forcibly the other way; she didn't seem to see why we shouldn't go on as before, would you believe? But enough of her—Helen,' he lowered his voice dramatically, 'has separated from Brian so I thought she could do with a little break.'

'Has she, now?' Mike said slowly. 'Tim——'

'Naturally she'd like to say hello—why don't you two come over for dinner?'

'I've got a better idea; why don't you and Helen join us?'

'Mike,' Sidonie said nervously some time after Tim had left, promising to be back within the hour, 'I don't think this is a very good idea.' It had been in her mind to say it as *soon* as Tim had left but she'd found herself curiously tongue-tied.

'Neither do I.' He was watching her batter some fish as he'd taught her. They'd both showered and changed and in clean shorts and a fresh white T-shirt moulded to the muscles of his broad shoulders and with his hair tidy and damp he took her breath away for a moment as she lifted her head to look at him anxiously. 'However,' he went on, 'we might as well get it over and done with. Tim won't leave us in peace until we do and, as you may have noticed, Pancake Creek is a hard place to dodge your friends. I also feel——' he moved his shoulders irritably '—as if I owe him one.'

'Well, I can understand that,' she said with a faintly tart edge that caused him to suppress a slight smile, 'but, apart from anything else, he doesn't know.'

'Know what?' he queried and removed a smudge of flour from the tip of her nose with his finger.

'About us,' she said hollowly.

'Then he soon will.'

Sidonie placed the last battered fillet of fish on the plate and turned away to rinse her hands. 'I don't think I want him to, though, Mike,' she said carefully. 'Which is why it might have been easier to go to their boat.'

He put his hands on her shoulders and turned her to face him so that he could look narrowly into her eyes. 'Why don't you want him to know?'

She couldn't help the tinge of pink that came to her cheeks or the tremor that ran through her body but she tried to marshal her thoughts against that narrowed, rather rapier-like blue gaze of his. 'For two reasons,' she said quietly at last. 'I'd rather what's between you and me stayed that way. It is something that's just between us, isn't it?' She swallowed.

He said after a long pause, 'Yes, put like that but——'

'No, Mike, listen to me,' she pleaded although a certain stubborn light had entered her grey eyes. 'That's the way I want it to stay. I don't want anyone else to——' her throat worked as she tried to express herself honestly yet in a way that staked no claims '—to trample through it even kind-heartedly as Tim might, although then again he might not. And that's my second reason—it could complicate things...' She broke off and looked up at him helplessly.

'As a matter of fact, Sidonie,' he said sombrely and moved his hands on her shoulders, 'it could uncomplicate things, if Tim still has hopes regarding Helen.'

'And if Helen still has hopes?' she whispered, her gaze steady but shadowed. 'No, Mike——' she shook her head and closed her eyes briefly '—don't use me to do that. Because that would flaw what has been something nearly perfect for me.'

His hands suddenly tightened on her until she winced and he said roughly, 'Sid, what do you think I am? I——'

But a dinghy bumped against the stern and Tim called, 'Ahoy there!' boisterously, as well as knocking ringingly against the planking of the hull. 'Anybody home?'

'*Mike*?' Sidonie said desperately. 'Please.'

'What about the *evidence* of it?' he said tersely and gestured towards the aft cabin. 'She's going to want to look around.'

'I've hidden it all.'

He stared down at her, his mouth set in a suddenly hard line, then he shrugged.

* * *

'It's lovely, Mike,' Helen said softly. She ran her fingers over the dining-table. 'Although I still have a soft spot for your first boat even though we had to rough it compared to this.'

And Sidonie knew suddenly, with a further sick feeling, that Helen had done this trip with Mike once. But that was the only reference the other girl made to things that had once been; otherwise she was the perfect guest, quietly intelligent, helpful and happy to let her brother do a lot of the talking. Yet, once you knew these two had loved each other, Sidonie thought with despair, you couldn't imagine it being any other way.

Not that Mike showed anything other than that Helen was a friend he appreciated. There was no stiffness in his manner, although she did see his eyes linger once on the faint pale band of skin where Helen's wedding-ring had obviously recently reposed. But for both of them, from what they said and the way they acted, it might simply have been a case of two friends meeting each other again after some time—might have been unless you *knew*. And of course Tim knew; it wasn't hard to see the way he watched them despite his antics—his antics which Sidonie found herself drawn into so as not to appear as what she was—a live-in lover aboard *Morning Mist*—with disastrous consequences.

'Now little Sid here,' Tim said, putting his arm about her shoulders after they'd finished the fish, 'is the kind of crewperson most men dream about. She can strip a diesel motor, Mike tells me, pop up a sail, read a GPS and radar as good as any man, besides being a very straight kind of girl—Karen shocked her to the core.'

Sidonie blushed and squirmed inwardly. Which caused Tim to laugh and say, 'Don't look like that; you showed more judgement than the rest of us. Wouldn't you say, Mike?'

'Yes,' Mike agreed, but drily.

'But tell me more,' Helen said with genuine interest. 'Where did you learn about diesels?'

'It was Sid's greatest ambition to work with motor-bikes once,' Mike said with a faint smile. 'She's an unusual girl.'

'I'm a bit of a freak actually,' Sidonie heard herself confiding. 'There are some things I'm terribly bad at——'

'She means she can't swim and she can't cook, otherwise she's quite normal,' Mike put in.

'But I'm learning, aren't I?' Sidonie replied with a touch of genuine reproach.

'Indeed you are,' he said gravely.

'And Mike actually found her on the dock at Airlie Beach!' Tim said jovially in what Sidonie realised was a clumsy attempt to establish her correct status on *Morning Mist*.

'Just like a waif and a stray,' she said brightly herself and immediately flinched inwardly but it was as if she were on a rollercoaster she couldn't get off. 'Here today, gone tomorrow, although it wasn't actually the dock, it was the main street. Mike, would you like me to clear the table and get the dessert?'

His eyes lingered on her enigmatically. 'No, you stay put, I'll do it,' he murmured.

'You don't look like a waif or a stray,' Helen said slowly, her beautiful hazel eyes showing concern, and she grimaced immediately. 'Forgive me, that sounds awful but——'

'I'm not really,' Sidonie said.

And Mike said over his shoulder at the same time, 'She isn't. She's also a Bachelor of Science and Arts and has been a wildly successful teacher—depending on whose point of view you take.'

'Curiouser and curiouser,' Helen said with just a hint of that heartbreakingly lovely smile. 'I'd love to hear more, Sid.'

Sidonie took a deep breath. 'Well, I went up to Airlie Beach to take up a teaching post as it happens, but in fact it didn't happen, to cut a long story short, and when...Mike was looking for crew I thought that instead of going straight back to Melbourne this would be like a holiday. That's all there really is to tell. I——'

But Tim leapt into the breach. 'And she's been like a favourite kid sister to us ever since! Here, let me top up the wine.'

Oh, Tim, Sidonie couldn't help herself thinking with a shaft of pain, have you forgotten that I traded confidences with you one night? I suppose it seemed so out of the question... And irrelevant, anyway, if these two are made for each other.

She struggled through another hour before the Molloys took their leave and was simply standing in the middle of the cabin when Mike came back from seeing them off.

'Sid?'

She lifted her shadowed, weary face to him. 'Yes, Mike?'

'Don't you honestly think that was all a little pointless?' He made no attempt to touch her.

She lifted her shoulders anguishedly. 'I don't *know*.'

'Then I'll tell you,' he said deliberately. 'There's no chance of Helen and me getting together again, because you can't change the basic things about yourself——'

'You don't know that, Mike,' she broke in huskily. 'She *may* have changed and come to understand . . . better. She doesn't look or sound like a . . . I don't know, the kind of person who *couldn't* understand you. If you must know,' she said barely audibly, 'you and she look as if you might have been made for each other.'

'Then looks can be deceiving,' he said harshly. 'Nor are you in any position to be an expert on the subject, so would you do me a favour and stop theorising as well as tormenting yourself unnecessarily? There's no need.'

'Unnecessarily?' she whispered, and found that her throat hurt with the effort to speak and her head hurt with the effort to think; but she knew she must, because the metaphorical train seemed to be gathering speed within her and rushing her to either of two unacceptable destinations: one where she would break her promise and break down and tell him that without him she would be tormented for the rest of her life; or the other—and her vague fears suddenly crystalised in her mind—where she would hear him suggest some compromise for them, some arrangement, although she couldn't think what, but mainly because he couldn't bring himself to abandon her like some stray . . . Why, oh, why did I *use* those stupid words? It's what's been worrying me since Rosslyn Bay.

'All right,' she said suddenly and tried to smile. 'No more—nonsense. Could we go to bed, please? Unless—you'd rather not.'

'Why not?'

'I don't know.' She bit her lip. 'I meant—rather not go to bed with *me*—oh, hell,' she said hopelessly, and added with bleak honesty, 'If you must know it's a little difficult to imagine you wanting to sleep with me—after her. She was so. . . elegant as well as everything else, someone who could grace the pages of *Vogue*, I'm sure,' she added with a prickle of sudden defiance.

He studied her in silence for a long moment. Then he picked up her hand and kissed her knuckles. 'Let me show you, then,' he murmured.

But he didn't make love to her; he held her instead and soothed her to sleep, stroking her hair as he often did. And even if she was glad, because nothing else would have seemed right to her overburdened spirit, she was also hauntingly sad.

She woke with her head on his shoulder, could hear the gentle slap of water against the hull and curled in even closer to him before she remembered and attempted to sit up abruptly.

'Don't.' He pulled her back.

'Mike——'

'Don't start, Sid,' he warned softly. 'Let's give ourselves a break.'

For once, she remained uncharacteristically silent. Until he said wryly, his hands roaming her warm, soft body gently, 'What are you thinking, sweet Sid?'

She grimaced, for in truth she had a jumble of thoughts going through her mind—that men really were incredible sometimes being one. That despite this she wasn't going to be able to resist him, that somehow or other she had to get her act together . . .

She said, 'Sometimes when you call me that you make me feel like sweet pea.'

He laughed quietly and pushed his hair out of his eyes then rubbed the blue shadows on his jaw. 'You remind me of a flower. I used to think it was a wild rose, thorny but worth the prickles. I can translate to a sweet pea easily, though. Fragrant——' he sniffed the silken hollows of her throat and lower '—delicate, a lovely blossom on a slender stem—yes, not hard at all.'

'I . . . really?' She couldn't help herself.

'Really and truly,' he vowed and moved aside the covers.

'Mike——'

'No, let me look at you, Sid.' And he drew his hand down her body. 'I sometimes think of that outfit you wore when we first met,' he went on, 'and what un-imagined delights it concealed. But then again I'm glad. It's been like a voyage of discovery.'

'Mike,' her voice shook, 'you say the nicest things sometimes.'

For a moment, though, as he stared down at her, she thought she saw something in his eyes that could have been pain. But he said, 'It's true.' And he started to make love to her.

Dear diary, we left Pancake Creek that morning. The wind had settled overnight to a steady ten knots so we put up the sails, said goodbye to Helen and Tim and got under way. I don't know why but my mem-ories of Pancake Creek will always be of a wise, ancient, timeless, serene sort of place—and that's really odd when you think of the turmoil I alone went through there. I'll also never forget Helen and Tim standing on the back of *Moonshine*, Tim with his arm round her shoulders as they waved us goodbye. And Mike ... never looking back once. I believe there's a cemetery near the lighthouse on Bustard Head with some very old graves; perhaps Pancake Creek has seen its fair share of suffering too ... Perhaps I too will be wise and serene because of it all one day, but to say that at the time I didn't know what to do would be to put it mildly, diary, only there wasn't a lot I could do then. That opportunity didn't come until a few days later.

They had a pleasant trip to Burnett Heads and then a rough trip across Hervey Bay.

'Which is a pity,' Mike said, putting his arm around her; 'I was hoping to show you some whales. I suppose you know all about the humpback whales and how they migrate annually from Antarctic waters up here to breed and have their young?'

'Tell me all the same,' Sidonie said. 'Have you seen any?'

'Last year I saw a mother and her calf not far from Rooney Point.' He pointed. 'That's the northern part of Fraser Island, the eastern arm of Hervey Bay. They played for nearly an hour. It was quite a sight. But you need patience and better conditions to find them. And time.'

Time, she thought, which is running out. Tin Can Bay, at the southern end of the Great Sandy Straits that divided the mainland from Fraser Island, was only a day away and she couldn't help herself from shivering suddenly.

Mike looked down at her. 'Cold?'

'A bit. Where will we anchor for the night?'

'I was thinking of North White Cliffs, in the straits. 'll give us a bit of protection from this southerly. 'e could even have a meal ashore; there's a new resort ere, Kingfisher Bay. I don't think it's quite finished ut I believe they're taking guests. How would that uit you, Miss Hill?'

'Just fine!' she responded. 'But I'll have to wash y hair.'

He laughed and ruffled her hair. 'Looks fine to me.'

She presented herself to him later in her special dress ith her hair all curly and squeaky clean. 'Will I do?'

'Very well. Will I?'

Her heart started to beat oddly as she pretended to spect him thoughtfully. He wore his jeans with a hite shirt open at the throat and a very fine, dark een pullover. 'You'll do,' she said in a strangely gruff tle voice. 'Let's go!'

'Hang on. You'll need a jumper. It's a lot cooler wn here.'

Her brow creased. 'I haven't really got one, not to with this dress.'

'Well, I'd better lend you one of mine; you can ng it over your shoulders,' he said, and a minute ter came back with a white one. 'There——' he aped it carefully around her '—what do you ckon?'

Sidonie closed her eyes for a moment and breathed his heady aroma that clung to the wool. But she id jauntily, 'I might even set a new fashion—who ows? Mike, I'm starving!' But she knew that she s forcing herself to be bright and jaunty, and won- red if she was fooling him.

It was hard to see much of the outside of the new ort in the dark but it obviously wasn't finished from

the construction materials and mounds of earth lyin
around on the walk up from the jetty. The mai
complex was finished, however, and it was not har
to see in the brightly lit restaurant that Mike attracte
no little attention, and the two of them together som
curious looks.

We probably do make an odd-looking coupl
Sidonie thought miserably as she ploughed her wa
through a large steak.

'Something wrong with it, Sid?'

'No, no!' She looked up anxiously.

'I thought you said you were starving.'

'I thought I was!'

'Leave it,' he said quietly. 'Have some wine. Yo
haven't touched it yet. And tell me why you're upse
Sid.'

She tensed and all but knocked the glass over a
she went to pick it up. 'I was hoping,' she said bleakl
as he steadied her hand around the stem of the glas
'you wouldn't notice. I was really hoping not to spo
our last night. I'm just being stupid.'

'Why do you imagine this is our last night, Sid?'

'Well, it's Tin Can Bay tomorrow; that's the en
of the line, isn't it?' She sipped some wine and hope
against hope it would steady her nerves.

'No, it's not. I thought we might go on t
Melbourne together.'

Her eyes widened and she stared at him over th
rim of her glass then took another hasty sip, whic
all but caused her to choke. 'S-so,' she said di
jointedly, 'that you can introduce me to a prospectiv
employer?'

'Something like that.' He lay back in his chair an
studied her thoughtfully. 'How would that suit you'

'It would be wonderful,' she said honestly,
ut——'

'Then let's do it,' he drawled.

'But...do you *have* to go to Melbourne? I wouldn't
ant to take you out of your way!'

He grimaced, his eyes never leaving her face. 'I
efinitely have to go to Melbourne and nothing you
an do or say will make me change my mind.'

Sidonie lowered her glass at last. 'Is there some-
ing I don't understand, Mike?'

'Possibly. I wouldn't worry about it, though.' His
ps twisted.

She eyed him uncertainly.

'So, while this might be our last night on *Morning
ist*, it's not our last night together. By any means,'
e added idly. 'Should we drink to that?' He raised
is glass.

Sidonie raised hers, but bemusedly.

want to tell you about Helen, Sid,' he said quietly,
ter, when they were stretched side by side in bed and
e cabin was dark.

'You don't have to——'

'Yes, I do; just be quiet and listen,' he said wryly.
he is a thoroughly nice person and we did have an
ffair but it got bogged down, as you probably know,
ver what I do. The mere thought of it genuinely
ightened her stiff—and it always will. She...came
verseas with me for a while; I thought it might help
she saw how mundane a lot of it really is—if any-
ing it made her worse and it affected my concen-
ation, knowing she was waiting on the ground biting
er nails mentally. Unfortunately, there was a crash

round the time she was there too. So she came home
I stayed on.

'That was the other problem—the fact that I worke
overseas. They're a very close family, the Molloys
and she found it hard to tear herself away from them
Now I'm sure you, Sid, would say that true love woul
find a way around all this—well, Helen and I couldn't
And it dragged on for a time then she marrie
someone else. That's all there is to it because, yo
see, nothing has changed despite the fact that he
marriage didn't work. I'm under contract for at leas
another five years, and I wouldn't want to be any othe
way.'

Sidonie opened her mouth to say, as she'd sai
before, that Helen *could* have changed. But she close
it and said instead, 'Thanks for telling me. But I'n
not really sure why you have.'

'You don't think that since you're sharing a be
with me you warrant some sort of explanation?' h
teased. 'Most girls when confronted with a
old . . . mistress do.'

'Ah, but I'm not most girls.' And none of that tell
me whether you can stop loving someone even if yo
can't work your life around it, she thought but didn'
say.

'I know, although I mistrust the way you say that
'Why?'

He thought for a bit then leant up on one elbov
and smoothed the collar of her pink pyjama-top abou
her throat. 'I get the feeling it could be the prelud
to a lengthy discourse on all sorts of things, the natur
of love and life among them. However, I have a bette
suggestion; should we just take things one day at
time for the moment and—see how we go?'

And that was when she knew with sudden certainty that Mike Brennan, who loved someone he couldn't have, was thinking of making do with second-best. Well,' she temporised with a tremor in her voice, perhaps you're right.'

'Right about what?' he enquired quizzically.

'That it wouldn't be a good idea to deliver myself of any lectures tonight. I must warn you that I could feel differently tomorrow, though——'

'I'd be surprised if you didn't. Go to sleep now.' He kissed her lips gently.

She fell asleep surprisingly quickly. But she woke much earlier than he did and lay for a long time watching the dawn illuminate his face, and knew that now was the time to make good her promise; she wasn't sure how, but it had to be done...

In fact it proved surprisingly easy. All she had to do was stow away on a boat...

She'd slipped out of bed before he woke and was pottering around the galley in a preoccupied, tense frame of mine when he came out of the aft cabin rubbing his hair and yawning.

'What's up?'

'Nothing. Just felt like getting up early.'

He switched on the radio. 'Any chance of a cup of tea?'

'Coming up!'

'It's a hive of activity around here,' he said, peering out of a porthole.

'Mmm. Barges coming and going—about half an hour ago a big catamaran dropped off hundreds— well, it looked like it—of workers. Building workers.' She stopped pouring the tea for a moment, her eyes widening, then resumed what she was doing carefully.

'Well, we can't go anywhere for a few hours un
fortunately.' He took a mug from her and sat dow
at the chart table and pulled the tide book toward
him. 'We need at least a half-tide to get through
few shallow spots.'

'I might—would you mind if I went ashore for
while, then, Mike?'

'Why not? I'll come with you. We can see the plac
in the daylight.'

She turned away from him and bit her lip but said
'Great!'

In the event things worked out her way, though
Mike went up top after breakfast, was recognised b
someone on another boat anchored close by, an ol
air force friend, and invited across for a chat. He cam
down grimacing. 'Do you want to come, Sid? Billy i
determined to have one of those ''Do you remembe
the time when'' we were young and foolish kind o
chats,' he said with a mixture of exasperation and af
fection. 'He's offered to pick me up in his dinghy s
you can still go ashore in ours if you want to.'

'Well,' Sidonie said slowly, her heart beating heavil
and a dew of cold sweat breaking out on her brow
'I would like to add Fraser Island to my list of th
places I've been, in the daylight... I have a menta
list, you see.' She gathered momentum. 'Sidonie Hi
stood here, kind of thing...' And ran out of steam

He laughed and kissed the top of her head. 'OK
you go and do it, Miss Livingstone. Just don't ge
entangled with any single mothers this time.'

'I won't,' she promised, and couldn't take her eye
off him as he climbed up the ladder and disappeare
through the hatch.

CHAPTER NINE

IT WAS a wet, typically Melbourne day two weeks later. Sidonie sat on a bus and watched an airliner gain height through a break in the clouds in the distance and wondered if Mike was on it. She clasped her hands in her lap and tried to control some foolish tears. Remember what you said in your note, she told herself—and that was not hard to do because the words seemed to have graven themselves on her heart...

> I wish I didn't have to do this, Mike, but it seems the only way. I feel horrible about lying to you but in my heart and soul I know I'm not the right one for you and the best way for both of us is a clean break. Please don't worry about me, I really am terribly resilient, and I'd much rather, when you thought of me, that it was with a bit of a smile— I'm leaving you my Edward Lear to help you along! I can't thank you enough for everything else—
>
> Sidonie

'And that's it, dear diary,' she said to herself. 'I've got myself a job—teaching again, twelve-year-olds this time, and I certainly won't be teaching them poker, although it's a bit of a dreary school in a dreary part of Melbourne—but no, I won't be tempted. And I've got myself a flat, of sorts——' she grimaced '—but once I get used to it and brighten it up a bit it'll be fine. So that really is it, diary! I won't be talking to you any more; that chapter of my life is closed and I can only go on to bigger and better things——'

'You all right, miss?'

'Oh.' Sidonie turned to the man who had sat down beside her without her realising it. 'Yes, really, fine, thank you! How are you?'

He stared at her and raised his eyebrows. 'Just thought, seeing as you were talking to yourself and crying at the same time, you might not be feeling the full quid.'

Sidonie dashed at her cheeks and was mortified to find them wet. 'Ah. Well, you see,' she said earnestly, 'I've just closed rather an *epic* chapter of my life—you wouldn't *believe* the adventures I had! But I'm also going on to fresh fields and—er—my stop is coming soon, I mustn't miss it! I managed to get a flat right opposite the bus stop, which I thought was rather convenient, don't you agree?' She stood up, peered through the rain and pressed the bell.

'Well, I'll tell you what I think,' the man said with a bit of a grin, 'you're sickening for something, love. Why don't you go home and go to bed?'

Sidonie cast him a speaking look as she squeezed past him but he only grinned more widely so she tossed her head and sprang off the bus with a fine disregard for the kerb——

So that when she landed she tripped on it and would have fallen had not a strong pair of arms caught her. At the same time a voice she knew well said savagely, 'You bloody idiot! I can't let you out of my sight!'

'Mike?' she whispered, going as pale as paper as she stared up into his furious blue eyes. 'How did you find me?'

He swore and said, 'Not with any help from you! Just tell me one thing—how *did* you get off that blasted island?'

'I . . .' she swallowed '. . . I stowed away.'

'You stowed away,' he repeated with the sort of rigid control that was actually frightening. 'What did you stow away on?'

'A—a barge. Wh-when they weren't looking,' she stammered, 'I hopped on and hid behind a big drum. Funnily enough it's the first time I've felt seasick in years but I think it might have had something to do with the fumes coming from the drum, some sort of kerosene——'

'Stop right there, Sidonie,' he ordered through his teeth. 'If you think you're going to talk your way out of this by talking twaddle, you're mistaken. Do you realise we all but scoured the whole of Fraser Island for you? Give me your key.'

And so overpowering was the force of his rage that she fumbled in her bag and produced it.

Two minutes later they were inside and he looked around sardonically. 'You call this being resilient?'

She bit her lip and began to take off her raincoat. 'It's only a start, Mike, and—what's wrong now?' she whispered as he turned that harsh blue gaze on her and it went even harsher if possible.

'I thought I told you never to wear those clothes again,' he said with soft menace.

'I . . .' She looked down at her cotton shirt and hound's-tooth skirt. 'They're practical and I can't quite afford yet to be blasé about clothes that still have a lot of wear left in them.'

'Oh, yes, you can,' he said, still with that harsh look, 'so we might as well start getting rid of them now.' And he strode towards her and started to unbutton her shirt.

'*Mike*...' Her eyes widened in horror as he flipped open the last button and slipped the offending shirt off her shoulders. Beneath it she wore a very plain, modest pale pink bra.

'Sidonie?' he replied, his eyes on it and the gentle curves beneath. Then he looked into her eyes. 'You asked me once about the deep, dark, brooding kind of passion that goes on between men and women, didn't you, Sid? Well, now you know—this is it.'

She licked her lips frantically. 'I don't know what you mean...'

'Don't you? Let me put it in question and answer form, then,' he said roughly. 'How the *hell* do you expect me to live the rest of my life without you?'

Her lips parted incredulously.

'I can't sleep, I'm overdue in the UK and all the while you've been merrily stowing away on barges and tripping on kerbstones—and you thought I could console myself with Edward Lear? You were wrong.' He pulled her into his arms and held her hard against him.

'Mike—Mike,' she said a bit later, 'I'm still not sure about this.'

He was seated in the only armchair the flat boasted and she was on his lap, cradled in his arms. He had kissed her forcefully and then with a deep sigh picked her up and carried her over to the chair.

'I might have known that,' he said ruefully. 'Don't you think I've gone through just about the full spectrum of emotions only a man in love can? Do you realise, Sid, that because of you I have a police record now?' he said gravely.

Her eyes were huge suddenly. 'Why?'

'Why do I have a record of being pathetically lunatic? I'll tell you why—I keep calling them up and getting them out to search for the same girl.'

'Oh, Mike,' she said contritely, 'I am sorry about that but I did leave you a note and—I just thought that if I didn't do it secretly—leave Fraser, I mean— you would catch up with me before I got very far away. You haven't——' a sudden thought struck her '—had them searching for me in *Melbourne*, have you?'

'No. I didn't think they'd be very co-operative.'

'Well, how did you find me? I've been very careful not to go back to the campus or the laboratory just in case.'

'Just in case I was looking for you?'

'Well . . .' she found she had to think that one out a bit '. . . I mean, it's not much good trying to make a *clean* break if one can be found easily, is it?'

'So you were really serious about never seeing me again, Sid?' he said quietly.

She took a breath. 'Don't think it was easy—I mean . . .' She trailed off and plucked at her skirt agitatedly. 'How *did* you find me?'

'Quite by accident. I was checking out my sea-phone account. It lists all the calls made from the boat item by item—number by number in other words—and because they once got mixed up and charged me for calls made from another boat I keep a record and check the bill against it. I came across this Melbourne number——'

'My friend's?' Sidonie said on a slow breath.

'Yes, the friend you rang from Hamilton, from the boat, to say you weren't coming after all. She gave me your address.'

'Oh. I didn't think of that.'

'I'm glad.'

'Mike—I still don't know what to do.' And her grey eyes were supremely distressed.

His lips twisted then he looked around and said wryly, 'Could we transport this conversation to somewhere more convivial, do you think?'

Sidonie looked around too and took a shuddery little breath but a spark of mutiny lit her eyes at the same time. 'I would have made it all right,' she said stubbornly. 'I would have been . . . OK.'

He looked down at her sombrely. 'Do you know, Sid, that's the stuff nightmares are made of for me now . . . ? Come, let's go somewhere warm.'

'I——'

But he set her on her feet and stood up himself, taking her hand. 'Bring your hat—you haven't lost your hat, have you?'

'Oh, no!' She looked shocked. 'Without it and——' She broke off and bit her lip.

He drove her away in what he told her was a hire car and took her to a hotel that was luxurious enough to make her eyes widen and to make her feel distinctly odd in her rather battered raincoat with her glorious hat in her hand.

And once up in his room he closed the curtains against the heavy, leaden dusk, lit some lamps and poured them a glass of wine each.

Sidonie took her raincoat off and hung it up carefully but in her mind were the words he'd said about nightmares, and the confusion they'd brought her—— Did he really mean . . . ? she wondered, and sat down equally carefully and accepted her glass from him. But, as she looked up at him to thank him, all the old uncertainties hit her again and added to them was a feeling of unfamiliarity. This Mike, soberly dressed in a beautifully cut charcoal suit that undoubtedly highlighted his broad shoulders, a pristine white shirt and discreet green and black silk tie, was like another person from another world, a sophisticated, monied world way out of her league and one that also evoked memories of Helen.

'I have to talk,' she said urgently.

He sat down opposite her and observed the way she sat, so upright, her knees pressed together, her glass held in both hands in her lap, and suppressed a slight smile. 'Go ahead,' he murmured. 'I'm not going to leap on you, Sid.'

She coloured. 'About Helen,' she said determinedly, however.

'What about her?'

But it wasn't so easy and she started a couple of times, stopped, then said helplessly, 'She's so elegant and lovely, so right for you and all this...' She waved a hand expressively and ran out of words.

'Sid,' he said quietly, 'I have to confess that I thought the same once——'

'Whereas I am——' new inspiration hit her and wouldn't be denied '—such a mass of ineptitudes, wrong clothes, crazy ideas——'

'Listen to me, Sid,' he said compellingly; 'those things don't mean a thing to me—in fact I like a lot of your crazy ideas——'

'But you don't like my clothes.'

'Not all of them. I like your special dress very much—I would even like you to wear it when we get married, and your hat——'

'*Mike* . . .' She spilled some wine in her lap as her whole body tensed convulsively.

But he said with a dry little smile, 'Keep listening, Sid—you brought this up so you owe it to me to finish it off. However lovely and elegant Helen is, the fact of the matter is also that she got transplanted in my heart by a pink and white slip of a girl, and there's not a damn thing I can do about it. Incidentally, she agrees with me.'

Sidonie's eyes widened. 'She knew?' she whispered.

'She knew,' he agreed. 'So all your precautions were unnecessary.'

'How?'

He shrugged. 'She must have picked up the vibes.'

'And how do you know all this, Mike?'

'I went to see her. She and Tim got back a few days ago. I felt I owed it to both of them to . . . explain. In the event it wasn't all that necessary. She said she'd guessed that night in Pancake Creek how I felt. She also said that no longer to have to feel guilty about walking out on me and marrying another man was a tremendous relief to her and that perhaps she'd been confusing the guilt with—other feelings for a long time.'

'Do you think that's true?' Sidonie stared at him like a wide-eyed little owl.

He moved his shoulders. 'I don't know but I very much hope that one day she finds someone to love as I have.' He looked down at his hands for a moment then up into her eyes and his were very steady and calm. 'Is there anything else you want to talk about?'

She looked down, realised she held a glass of wine and suddenly raised it to her lips and took a deep draught.

'Because if not, may I catalogue why I can't get you out of my mind or my heart, Sid? And why I have nightmares?'

'I—I can't believe this is happening to me,' she stammered. 'You see, I find it so hard to visualise us—married. Perhaps I mean *me* married—I've got the feeling I'd be an unsuitable wife, especially for you.' She blinked several times. 'You know what a disaster I am in lots of respects——'

'Not those that matter; the rest I can cope with easily—so long as I know where you are,' he added with his lips quirking. 'But can I begin?'

She could only stare helplessly at him.

'In the first place,' he said, 'you're the only girl I've ever met who is as excited about my job as I am— for that matter who even understands anything about it, so it would be fair to say we have a true meeting of the minds in that respect that would be highly suitable, don't you agree?'

'Well . . .'

'In the second place, I can't think of anyone I would rather have to be the mother of my kids——'

'Mike, I might be *hopeless* with babies,' she rushed in.

'No, you won't,' he contradicted. 'Just think of them as little combustion engines—once you understand the mechanics of them, you'll be fine. For the rest of it, they'll have so much fun with you it will all take care of itself. Thirdly——' he ticked off a finger then looked into her eyes with an intensity that stunned her '—I cannot bear the thought of any other man sleeping with you or loving you or even touching you or you touching them and perhaps doing the things *I* taught you; I've never been so lonely in my

life as I have since you left, and you know, Sid, despite what you might like to think, we can philos-
ophise until the cows come home but the simple fact
is I *love* you and if we don't know why or how then
we'll just have to put it down to you . . . being *you*.'

'Oh, Mike,' she whispered and brushed away some
tears, 'that was so lovely but——'

'It was also true. Sid—there are any number of elegant girls out there but there's only one you.'

'But are you *sure* you don't feel fatherly and a bit
protective and are you *sure* that because I can understand limiting Mach numbers and things like that it
mightn't be . . . well, expedient to marry someone like
me?'

'Sid—look, let's deal with this once and for all. I . . .'
he paused ' . . . *you* seem to have this inflated opinion
of me which in fact I find rather wounding.' He
grimaced.

'What's that?' She frowned.

'Well, you treat me like some macho hero who can
only be satisfied by a stereotyped, much hackneyed
version of feminine perfection, and I'm not accusing
Helen of that but *you* don't know anything about her
other than that she's conventionally beautiful—I find
that rather discriminatory and chauvinistic to be
honest.'

'Are you calling me a chauvinist?' she said
uncertainly.

'Why not? The word actually means extremism and
has only latterly become a purely male attribute. What
I mean in *your* respect is that you demean me when
you try to tell me I can't possibly have fallen in love
with a girl who, thank God, is not a stereotyped,
hackneyed version of feminine perfection but who is,

to my eyes, as lovely and natural as a flower, as honest as the day is long, who is brave and intelligent, who never bores me and who, if she isn't in my bed, makes it feel like a desolate wasteland. Is that what you're accusing me of, Sid? I know, I know I probably gave you cause to think that once but——' his mouth twisted and his eyes were curiously bleak '—is that what you really think of me now?'

Sidonie put her glass down carefully then she got up swiftly and tumbled on to her knees in front of him. 'Oh, Mike,' she whispered, her heart beating suddenly in a way she'd never known, 'I think you mean it...'

'Sid——' he took her face gently in his hands '—that's what my nightmares are all about—that I won't be able to get you to believe it. That that wonderful, gallant, independent spirit of yours wouldn't accept it because of all the stupid things I did when I didn't know that I couldn't live without you. Even when, the day before you left, I was still...dithering about because...' He stopped and sighed.

'Mike, I don't think you have to go on,' she said. 'I——'

'Yes, I do.' His voice was suddenly grim and her eyes widened. 'Let me tell you it all so there can be no further misunderstandings... I had, after Helen, barred myself, you might say, from falling in love again and that's why it took me so long to understand what started to happen to me when you came into my life. But I should have known for a variety of reasons; I should have known when I was moved to make that...statement with Karen.'

Sidonie moved but his fingers remained very gently cupping her face.

'I should have known then that it wasn't just a rather brutal and cynical exercise because she was so blatant about it; I should have realised I was also saying to you, "Oh, no, little girl",' his voice dropped, '"I can't let you into my heart because I'm afraid of what might happen". I should have known——' he moved his thumbs gently on her cheeks as some tears started to fall '—when I couldn't—not make love to you. Oh, I told myself that perhaps I could turn it into a self-esteem-building process for you; I told myself I might leave you feeling like a freak if I didn't—but the truth of the matter was, I couldn't help myself, I wanted you, I *loved* your unique mixture of innocence and wisdom, and never more so than that morning when you were . . . just so honest and so loving yourself.'

'Mike,' she breathed.

'Hang on, I haven't finished yet.' His lips twisted. 'Then we came to Pancake Creek, and Helen was there and I realised suddenly that all the bitterness and pain had gone, and I began to see that if I couldn't have *you* what had happened with Helen would seem like child's play. I began to see that unlike Helen I had *never* been able to stand seeing you walk away from me, that I got quite demented if I thought I'd lost you and I didn't have you to teach things to, to get angry with——' he grimaced '—and to see that without you to be with me life wasn't going to be worth much at all but—Sid, the other crunch hadn't changed, you see.' His fingers moved on her face and he looked deep into her eyes. 'I know, we both know that it doesn't frighten you, what I do, and that you can take a realistic view of it, but there is still an element of danger in it that can put enormous strain on a wife. I've seen it so many times, in other marriages that have appeared to start out so well. And that's why I didn't do what I really wanted to do after Pancake Creek—which was handcuff you to me until I could find someone to marry us.'

'Oh, Mike...' her mouth trembled but there were stars in her eyes '... I can only say, again, that if you weren't happy I couldn't be happy; it just seems to be the way I'm made.'

'Now will you marry me, Sid?'

'Yes, Mike,' she said tremulously, 'only I didn't bring my dress with me.'

He laughed quietly. 'We can go and get it.' And he took her slender, naked body into his arms and rubbed his chin on her head. 'Feeling OK?'

'Yes. Why?' she asked softly.

'I've got the feeling I got a bit carried away.'

She thought of his intense lovemaking that had been so different from the gentleness and restraint he'd always used before—as if he hadn't been able to help himself—and smiled a wise, secret little smile against his chest. Because it had resolved her one last lingering doubt—the doubt that he could ever hunger for her in this way; it had quite routed her fish and chips theory, in fact.

'No,' she said seriously and moved away but linked her arms round his neck and let just her nipples brush the hard wall of his chest. 'I liked it,' she added consideringly. 'It gave me the feeling that I'd progressed up to Dover sole, you see, even beyond perhaps. Would it be too much to say that I've come as far as—lobster?'

He laughed and kissed her throat and drew his hands down her slim length as if he couldn't quite believe she was real, then wrapped her tight in his arms. 'Sid, sweet Sid,' he murmured huskily and she felt that hunger in him again, 'lobster, champagne and far beyond—just promise me one thing: don't ever run away from me again.'

'No, Mike,' she said obediently and clung close to him, trembling in his arms as a sort of nervous reaction started to set in.

'Hush, sweetheart,' he soothed.

'It's just that it's like all my dreams come true,' she whispered. 'I haven't had a chance to tell you that yet or tell you that I'm not so brave and all the things you said about me. I was actually scared stiff and lonely too and . . . bereft.'

He kissed her eyelids. 'We make a fine pair, then. My darling Sid, you're safe now. And so am *I*.'

'Is that how you really feel?' She couldn't help looking wonderingly into his eyes. 'I thought it was only me . . .'

'I know what you thought, but the truth is you're my safe harbour more than you'll probably ever know. You've released me from all the darkness you saw so accurately in me.'

'Mike,' she whispered, 'that makes me feel so wonderful.'

'Good,' he said wryly, 'then no more worries about being an unsuitable wife, because *no one* could suit me better. It's been like a . . . true voyage of discovery, reverting to nautical terms. And I won't rest easy until I *know* you believe me.'

So she tried to show him.

But two days later at their marriage ceremony, when he'd put a ring on her finger, she said solemnly, 'I've got something for you, Mike. You may not have missed it but I took this when I ran away, as a keepsake, and I slept with it next to my heart all the time we were apart; it was the only way I survived those days—I know it may not show you I suddenly believe I'll transform into a suitable wife but it will show how much I *love* you.'

He looked down at his red bandanna in her hands then swept her into his arms as if he'd never let her go.

'Er——' The marriage celebrant cleared his throat then shrugged and resigned himself to wait.

'Had this couple today,' he said to his wife later, 'who acted rather strangely. She gave him a scarf, not a new one either—quite a faded old one, in fact—and after he'd stopped kissing her, which took a long time, believe me, and despite the fact he was really well dressed—good suit and so on, and looked a regular sort of guy—he tied it round his head.'

'Takes all kinds, dear,' his wife said wisely.

Take 4 bestselling love stories FREE

Plus get a FREE surprise gift!

HARLEQUIN PRESENTS®

The Heat is On!

Watch out for stories that will
get your temperature rising....

They're

TOO HOT TO HANDLE

Coming next month:

Savage Destiny by Amanda Browning

Harlequin Presents #1724

Was he just using her?
Five years ago, Pierce had married Alix one day—
and rejected her the next. Once was enough for
Alix—she'd been burned. But then came a new dilemma....
She had to marry Pierce again for the sake of her family,
But this time she wouldn't suffer—even if Pierce was
still too hot to handle!

Available in February, wherever Harlequin books are sold.

THTH-1